BHAIRAVI: THE RUNAWAY

BHAIRAVI: THE RUNAWAY

Shivani

Translated from Hindi by
Priyanka Sarkar

SIMON & SCHUSTER
London · New York · Sydney · Toronto · New Delhi
A CBS COMPANY

YODAPRESS

First published in India by Simon & Schuster India, 2020
A CBS company and Yoda Press, New Delhi

1 3 5 7 9 10 8 6 4 2

Simon & Schuster India
818, Indraprakash Building,
21, Barakhamba Road,
New Delhi 110001
www.simonandschuster.co.in

Yoda Press
79 Gulmohar Enclave
New Delhi 110049
www.yodapress.co.in

PB ISBN: 978-81-946464-4-0
eBook ISBN: 978-81-946464-5-7

Typeset in India by SŪRYA, New Delhi

Printed and bound in India by Replika Press Pvt. Ltd.

MIX
Paper from responsible sources
FSC® C016779

Simon & Schuster India is committed to sourcing paper that is made from wood grown in sustainable forests and support the Forest Stewardship Council, the leading international forest certification organisation. Our books displaying the FSC logo are printed on FSC certified paper.

FOREWORD

Bhairavi is perhaps the darkest of my mother's novels. It was first serialized in the popular Hindi weekly *Saptahik Hindustan*, and published soon thereafter in 1978 by *Shabdkar Prakashan*. Once that publishing house closed down, it was published with most of Shivani's books by Saraswati Vihar Prakashan and ultimately by Radha Krishna Prakashan. They have published *Bhairavi* in both hard cover and paperback editions.

The late 1980s were a strange time in Independent India's history. The vernacular publishing industry had come of age and Hindi writers had found millions of readers across the Hindi belt. But at the same time royalties remain poor and publishers skittish. Also a new backlash of social conservatism was becoming visible on the horizon. It was hostile to women who had grown up in Gandhi, Tagore and Sarojini Naidu's liberal India, particularly those who wrote or performed on stage. Our tiny Kumaoni society of Chauthani Brahmins was no exception. Shivani's own family did not fit the joint family pattern, but the Brahminical ideology of the basic patrilineal system Brahmins in the hills lived by, eyed the Shantiniketan-educated Gaura Pant 'Shivani' with certain misgivings as an aberration. They were mystified and upset in equal measure by her prolific writing skills that made her into a great literary phenomenon with no help from either a literary mentor or the family. They criticized her in low tones but all read her work avidly as soon as it saw print. Later their mutterings that filtered down to us, courtesy of various aunts and uncles, were tinged with both a deep disapprobation and envy.

Some ideas are not new, but need to be affirmed by creative writers. Freedom of expression for women was one such. For our mother it meant not just continuing to write, but also sending all three of her daughters to college and introducing them to the world of creative writing, music, fine arts and of course numerous well-known writers.

By the time *Bhairavi* was published, Shivani's two older daughters had married into socially certified 'good families' to enviably promising young men. Another daughter and her only son were away in college and doing very well. But as in *Bhairavi*, behind this façade of joy darker shadows lurked unseen. Her son had just entered the IIT, the youngest daughter was to be married next year into a good family. But her husband who was about to retire, was quietly struggling with an illness he tried his best to downplay, but no longer could. Joy surrounded the house as the young engaged couple shot in and out, tailors and jewellers and aunts and uncles sat and made lists of chores to be completed, but one look at my father's steadily shrinking frame and mother knew this joyous occasion for her would be a precarious perch at best.

Bhairavi, written under these circumstances, has been both praised and attacked for its odd fangled and ambivalent approach to young life and the dark phenomenon of death, for the oddly mixed cultural background this saga presents the Hindi readers with: romantic love and sudden bereavement, ritualistic restraints of a middle-class life and the loosening of bonds among simple noble tribals. Tantra and sex among wandering bands of male and female Aghori ascetics people had long whispered about, but they were seldom reported in literature, least of all by a woman. Death, Walter Benjamin said once, is the sanction of everything a writer can tell. It confers upon a writer the responsibility to tell it like it is. And in *Bhairavi* Shivani did just that.

As a child I had noticed our mother's strange and simultaneous fascination for and revulsion from death rituals and cremations. If we were walking together and came across a group carrying a dead body draped in white on a bier, she grew pale and sat down wherever she was. A while later she'd gather herself and yell at us to get a move on, not gape at her like dimwits. It was much later when I re-read *Bhairavi* as an adult, that I realized how death that had stalked Mother's life, had shaped this book. Like Velazquez's court dwarfs, she and her siblings and their mother had had a ring side seat at the spectacle of worldly power and great wealth marred by death again and again.

While still in her teens Shivani lost her father, her eldest brother-in-law, and a few years later, her brother and mentor Tribhi. Her father's death had diminished their fortunes, complicated their lives and forced Shivani's large family to move to the hills where they faced a hugely conservative and judgemental community of high-bred Brahmins. After a few harrowing months there, they moved back to a better life in the royal palaces of Orchha, where the eldest son Tribhi was appointed the Prime Minister to His Highness of Orchha. Her brother and mother, however, saw to it that Shivani who was a brilliant student, graduated from Shantiniketan. Soon after this, a furious search was mounted in their own community to find a groom for, in my grandmother's words, 'this stubborn and powerful filly'. Shivani, then Gaura, was thus married off to my father, a widowed school teacher still mourning his beloved wife, and moved first to the tiny town of Jhansi, then back to the hills. All this had the effect of bringing Shivani's writings to focus steadily on the constantly shifting boundaries between cultures, between affluence and a genteel poverty, between the holy and the unholy and profane. She also realized how in her own life, the dead would never quite die but walk alongside as living memories, and often articulate their unfulfilled and angry desires through the living ones.

In *Bhairavi*, the young protagonist Chandan becomes a prism through whom Shivani the writer observes, watches, recognizes, listens to all this. What happens to an innocent fatherless young girl when Fate suddenly catapults her into a landscape totally exterior to her, not just once but again and again. Like the writer, Chandan has grown up far away from her natal community in a border town among children of the tribal Shauka people. This carefree innocent young girl is quite unaware of the big world outside, or her mother's reasons for her self-exile. Suddenly married off into a rich modern family far away in the plains, she tries hard to adjust to an entirely new life. But just when she is settling in, an accident throws her into another new world: a world free of sexual hierarchies, where a wandering band of Aghori Tantriks performs strange secret rituals in dark cremation grounds and forests. Male sexual prerogatives, prescriptive heterosexuality, women's inequality or the linking of sex with procreativity, all that Chandan had known, have all been discarded here amid the fumes of Ganja and Charas and alcohol deemed Prasad.

The road already travelled curls up behind Chandan, rolls up like a film as she stands ragged in ochre sari, amid burning pyres and a Ganja-smoking guru and his dubiously androgynous female chelis puffing away at their chillums. *Bhairavi* encapsulates the peculiar vital wisdom we dub as 'experience', when suddenly one's past is behind her and counts for nothing. Yet neither she nor her creator judge or turn a cynical eye. Chandan becomes a compassionate witness-cum-narrator of millions of unknown lives that are lived in this vast land, on the edges of the known society. Life thus revealed is an enigma. It fits no known social norms of the traditional society where each new encounter ends with a question mark and any answer immediately uncovers another question. Standing amid burning pyres, holed up in distant hovels with the guru's Dhooni and strange coming and goings at midnight, Chandan observes life as life might observe itself as a series of confessions and memories, interspersed with fragments of autobiographical fantasy.

To understand the timeless appeal of Shivani's fiction across decades her new readers must allow an ambivalent space for a woman writer's experience of life half a century ago. It is a world in which Chandan is sometimes Shivani, and at others not Shivani at all. But in her is enshrined a strange taste of freedom for women who got to live their life again and again by default as it were, with their past wiped clean.

My father passed away a year after *Bhairavi* was published. My mother was widowed with meagre savings, a son who was still in college and with no roof over her head. She, however, kept her head high and for the next thirty odd years lived in a flat rented from the government and continued to write. As her reader and daughter, I meet her countless admirers all over the globe. Among them there are simple housewives and professional men and women, school kids, and a surprisingly large number of diaspora Indians from India's Hindi belt, who confess they developed a taste for Hindi after reading Shivani's books . All of them confide how their mother, or grandmother or even great grandmother had first introduced them to Shivani's writings and once into it they were hooked for life.

Women writers who have this sort of strange freedom thrust on them, mostly resolve their tensions in laughter and in prose and in doing so they will, almost inadvertently, confer the gift of free thinking on their daughters. I learnt from Shivani both as mother and reader, that women leading socially secure lives as mothers and wives are not morally more credible or more capable than those who are without family or child. Till the end, Shivani remained a kaleidoscopic character for me: outwardly traditional but bold, perverse, un-beholden and totally free when she puts pen to paper. Reading *Bhairavi* and the strange composure and compassion in these pages that co-exists with pain and hurt, I feel it is not the moralist's why, but a humane what, that the writer ekes out from life, holds tenderly and finally redeems from oblivion.

Mrinal Pande
24 May 2020

PREFACE

It was the summer of '97. I was all of 14 and restless, guilt-tripping my single mother for yet another summer vacation wasted in the sweltering small town of Udaipur when we could have had gone somewhere exciting and cooler. Exasperated, Ma pushed a copy of Shivani's *Surangama* into my hand.

I knew nothing about Shivani at that point but *Surangama* drew me in. Her story spoke to me at a personal level though there were parts of the story that were beyond my understanding at that time. I gave my copy to my closest friend, convincing her to read it, and went back to raid Ma's library and read whatever I could find by Shivani. I was drawn into her small-town world of the hills, a world I was somewhat familiar with. Her heroines were all beautiful, independent, talented and strong-willed. They fucked up or life fucked them up but they persevered. I wanted to be them.

Twenty-three years have passed since then. I got out of the small town, got a college education in the big city, then went on to work in publishing, living a life more or less on my own terms. At a personal level, I realize that I got to do and be a lot of things that Shivani's heroines didn't even get the chance to do. She was writing between the 1950s and 1970s. Times have changed somewhat—I am living in a big city and have many freedoms—though that is probably the oversimplification of the century.

Gaura Pant urf Shivani's stories, characters and the situations they find themselves in still resonate for me; at times they can even be triggering. What makes her stories so powerful other than her characters, is her vivid writing that had made her a household darling in the Hindi-reading belt of India. Her readers were primarily women. That could be because she was writing about the home and the hearth and the sense and sensibilities of those within it.

One of the reasons she wasn't as celebrated and fêted like her contemporaries were, despite being to every Hindi-reading woman in the country what Uttam Kumar was to Bengali women, was that she was seen as a writer of 'love stories' and not a chronicler of society. We know how Jane Austen was regarded by her contemporaries and how 'chick-lit' is viewed by the literati today. Stories, no matter how authentic the accounts are, about women coming from a certain class and born with certain privileges, have often been disparaged by the largely male literati of different eras, and Shivani's experience was no different. She received a Padma Shri almost towards the end of her life. Even now, very few courses in universities include her works in their syllabi.

Shivani's stories are set in the locale she was most familiar with, the Kumaon hills, and her characters are mostly a product of their situations or middle-class conditioning. Her stories have some stock characters, the strong female lead and the wimpy, privileged love interest to whom you would want to give a good walloping. Then, there are one or more nemesis, mostly women, and they are largely a product of society and its expectations. There is a focus on the characters (mostly the men, all handsome but 'lily-livered') not being able to cope.

In *Bhairavi*, her fourth novel written in the 1960s, we meet such people too. Chandan begins as the perfect embodiment of what patriarchy desires from a woman. So meek that the narrator keeps calling her a 'cow' (translated as 'lamb' in the text), so virtuous that she is willing to risk life and limb every time her virtue is at risk, her beauty, rather her 'fairness', a mirror to her heart. However, this wet dream of every Indian man, though dutifully married off, is not rewarded at the end and instead ends up lost. Almost as if the author were saying, women can keep trying, but what options do they have in reality?

Then, there's Chandan's mother, Rajrajeshwari who for me is a far more interesting character. One youthful trespass and she has to live through hell—an emotionally abusive marriage that makes her so bitter that she wants to control every aspect of her daughter's life. This control leads to Chandan growing up in a claustrophobic, sheltered existence nobody should envy because it would do anyone more harm than good. Many parents continue to be guilty of this even today and perhaps *Bhairavi* can be seen as a 'how not to parent' guide for them. Shivani, with her ironic sense of humour, could well have been doing precisely that.

There are many other interesting characters in *Bhairavi*: the dark-complexioned, orphaned Charan for one, who has lived a life very different from Chandan's and manages to make the most of it. She along with her mentor and mother-figure Maya Didi educate Chandan about the ways of the world. Chandan's husband is credited with 'educating' her in the novel, but her real education begins only in the ashram, which is no less than a gothic manor, complete with fearsome pets and a handsome devil of a lord. There are funeral pyres, skulls and bones, snakes, dead bodies and a whole lot of hocus-pocus. In some ways, *Bhairavi* is Shivani's *Northanger Abbey*. Apart from the Austen vibes, Shivani was also deeply influenced by Daphne du Maurier, the queen of the modern gothic, as her daughter Ira once told me.

The real horror, however, emerges in the novel from the realities of life. A woman who has to eat food from a plate that her husband has spat in. Another who watches in horror as the man for whom she left everything behind turns out to be a potential violator, and hence spends her dying breaths trying to save another woman from him. Or the end of the story, where our heroine is left all alone without any support or shelter and in the grips of an addiction. The penultimate question that Chandan asks herself is really for the reader. Where really can a beautiful, young, addict of a woman without much of an education go?

However, there are certain issues that will be bothersome for a 21st-century reader. The constant equating of fairness and beauty, and therefore with a purity of character, at times grates on our nerves. Women who smoke, dress in western clothes and are sexually active are shown as being weak in character. Considering how the writer problematizes Rajrajeshwari and gently mocks the judgements about values and clothing emanating from her, one wonders whether Shivani problematized her own judgement of other characters. However, the novel stresses on Rajrajeshwari and Chandan being paragons and the other women being simply incompetent, so perhaps Shivani too had a blind spot.

While retellings of Western classics are much in vogue in these times, through cinema and animation, we have almost none for the works of popular Indian writers. If I were doing a retelling of *Bhairavi* for today's readers, I'd probably have had Chandan move into the devilishly handsome Guruji's bat-cave of her own volition and make exciting, slightly BDSM-y love with him, and then focus on the larger problem, of earning her own keep. Maya Didi could have been the ultimate dominatrix, she sure has that vibe about her. Or to go further back I would have made sure that Rajrajeshwari did not have to live her entire life paying for one mistake, and instead perhaps she could have had her mother shield her.

Charan is my favourite character though. The wild child could be re-imagined as a fantastical superheroine, an Amazonian warrior. Daughter of the forest and night, she battles trolls, gnomes, goblins, djinns, hunters and poachers alike. Her mad friend's 'special tea' is actually a potion that sharpens her skills. Her name is anathema to anyone who tries to profit from the forest. She is the reason why their neck of the forest is still as thick as it was in the 1950s. Our Chandan gets besotted with her and joins Charan as a fighter and lover.

The guru's charms have gotten old by now. Mystique can only take you so far, after all. The rejected lover goes back to Maya Didi but she rebuffs him and tells him that she has taken over his ashram and practice. She has her posse of submissives, so thanks but no thanks. He leaves for the shamshan and takes Samadhi there. That would have been my modern retelling.

I feel like I owe Shivani a debt for how her characters have shaped me. Shivani's spirit would have haunted me, in keeping with the theme of the story, had Ira Pande not let me anywhere near any of her mother's writings. Or had both Ira and Mrinal not helped me immensely by sharing material on Shivani's writing that wasn't available anywhere.

Or if Arpita Das, editor extraordinaire of Yoda Press, and their publishing partner Simon and Schuster had shoo-ed me away. Or later, Sangam House and Arshia Sattar (the conversations with her were a big help!) had not allowed me to darken their doorstep where I worked on this translation.

Or had Anish Chandy, Dibyajyoti Sarma and Saumya Agarwal not supported me through the process of being an editor-translator. And if my own mother had disowned me for not being able to do justice to the original work. But they did not, dear reader, so I can offer this translation for your delectation, and sleep peacefully at night.

TRANSLATOR'S NOTE

This is a translation and not a retelling.

The inconsistencies and omissions of the original have been retained. The original does not always mention the names at the outset and sometimes it isn't clear who is being spoken of or even who is speaking. Characters are introduced as someone's mother or brother or grandfather and it is only much later that their names are provided.

The protagonist's mother is sometimes called Rajrajeshwari and sometimes Rajeshwari. Rajeshwari's father is referred to as her father or Chandan's Nana for quite a while before we find out that his name is Mahim. Or that his former lover's name is Rampyari. This was perhaps to show the universality of certain emotions or expressions or to tell readers that what they went through is more important than who they are. Having said that, there are some obvious inconsistencies in the character arcs too. That is probably because the stories were serialized. A certain claim is made about a character, which is later refuted. The guru is built up as this mysterious, handsome man but is reduced to a creepy middle-aged man by the end of the story. It is mentioned that Rajrajeshwari has trained herself to be docile but turns out to be anything but that. A little unsure like most single mothers but definitely no lamb.

The original was not broken up into chapters. However, for the sake of readability, the story has been broken down into chapters.

In the translation I try to stay as close to the original as possible, and most of all, it was my intention to help the reader soak in the nuances of Shivani's incandescent prose. Dealing with these inconsistencies while doing the translation made it feel almost like a conversation with the original, as if I were asking the author—is this what you meant?

Shivani's writing is Sanskritized, interspersed with Urdu, Bangla and Kumaoni words—languages she had grown up with. Her prose is such that every word is a step that can lead you to a bend which can transport you from a desert to a sea. There's a fair bit of anthropomorphism. Take for example this line in the very first paragraph of *Bhairavi*, where she writes while setting the scene:

> 'Kya inn vrikshon ki patiyaan bhi, aranya ki mool bhayavahata se sahamkar hilna bhool gayi thi'n?'
>
> Translation: 'Have their leaves too forgotten to stir in fear of the jungle?'

Wherever possible, any deviations from the Sanskritized Hindi have been marked. Two characters, Maya Didi and Charan speak to each other in Bangla, a language Shivani was conversant in. Maya Didi in fact, speaks a dialect of Bangla. In the last conversation between Charan and Chandan, when Charan tells Chandan about her plans, she calls her husband 'hujband' while the rest of her dialogue is in regular Hindi. The texts the guru gave Chandan were in English but written in the Devnagari script. Marking these deviations interfered with the flow of the story and were hence not done.

There is a lot of word play and humour in the writing that I have had to recast to generate the same sense in the translation.

The untranslateable has been left as is and explained wherever possible. In other places, the hope is that the context will explain the meaning to readers.

Ultimately, the hope behind undertaking the translation is to familiarize young readers with Shivani's enduring stories and give them a taste of the craft and sensibility of this very popular writer.

ONE

It seemed as if the blue of the sky had ripped through the jungle to touch the earth. Old trees and fig trees stood silent and motionless like hermits. She had been staring at those trees for a while through the open window. Have their leaves too forgotten to stir in fear of the jungle? She tried to turn on her side. Every part of her body ached at the barest movement. A moan escaped her lips. On hearing the same pained breath from the day of the accident, an old fat woman jumped down from a bed in some dark corner of the room and bent over her.

That old hag murmured 'Jai Guru! Jai Guru!' and put her face so close to her that the reek of tobacco hit her like that of a pungent incense stick and woke her from her stupor. Shrinking from the odour, she closed her eyes and pretended to be unconscious. The old sanyasini went back to her dark corner as she continued her babble.

Uff! The sanyasini had such a terrible countenance. She was wearing a man's dhoti tied so high that it hung just below her knees. She had wrapped the end around her enormous stomach. Her breasts and stomach seemed to hang in layers and her bare breasts were covered in blood-red sandalwood paste, the redness of which had also brightened up her face. On the one hand, the unbearable pain in her back and on the other, the abominable appearance of the sanyasini! Her eyes were closed but for how long could she escape her reality? Will she have to spend her entire pointless existence surrounded by such ugly runaways? And the impersonal stillness of the dark room was enough to strangle her. After all, she was not in a room but what felt like a cave in the shape of a closed goods train. One wall had been carved to fashion a small window. The window was also such that it would summon a fresh breath of air with great gusto and then the next minute shut its ramshackle doors with equal enthusiasm to block the next gust. At times, the strong smell of the incense burning in the room threatened to choke her; Chandan wanted to run away. But, how could she?

That day, her helpless sob struck against the low roof of the cave turning it into an echo, and that terrible-looking Vaishnavi bent over her tear-stained face and then ran outside. After a while she heard many voices, but clenching her jaw, she lay there with her eyes closed. The low moonlight that had seeped through the clouds fell on her haggard face. If you looked closely, you could see the tearstains at the corners of her large eyes.

'See, she has regained consciousness. Had she not, would the tears have been there? I heard her moan twice.' The same sanyasini was saying, 'I think she might have internal injuries. It has been eight days; she hasn't taken even a sip of water. We should borrow a car and take her to the hospital in the city…'

'No!' A stern voice rang out like a blow on a kettledrum, 'she will not die.' 'Jai Guru, Jai Guru!' the sanyasini started saying, 'Can the words of the guru ever turn out to be false? Here, take the chillum that Charan has just filled, you should rest. I am sitting near her anyway, when you have said she won't die, then there is nothing to fear.'

'Why Charan? Have you forgotten to fill the chillum?' Exhausted, the guru demanded a drag of the chillum from Charan.

'How can she forget? Actually, we beat her up today.' The sanyasini put her large palms on the bed.

'Why? Has she stolen my stash again?'

'What else! I had counted the five lots that I had made. When I went to fill your chillum today, I found only three and realized what must have happened. When I stared at her in the light of the day, she turned red and the thief was caught. Hasn't even turned seventeen and she wants to smoke marijuana, and the guru's at that. I pinched her back three times and so hard that the guru's trident has formed there.'

'Ok, ok, go and sleep now, it is not good to assault anyone, Maya! Go, sleep now, Raghav has called me. Some Ramdasi Kirtaniya, has come from Burdwan. I'll be back tomorrow.'

The guru's voice was heavy with intoxication.

The sound of fading footsteps assured Chandan of the guru's departure even though her eyes were closed. The Vaishnavi got up from the bed and as soon as she did so, the bed that had sagged under her weight regained its balance. The lightweight Chandan who had felt like she had been under water came up for air. After a bit, the sound of the Vaishnavi's snores reassured her and she opened her eyes. The room was awash with moonlight, as if dipped in it. A blast of cool air alerted her senses. She inspected the room carefully for the first time. Such a low ceiling! She felt like she could touch the wooden beam if she only stretched her hand. Several saffron potlis hung from the smoke-blackened wood of the thick beams; saffron dhotis and a few rudraksha necklaces with big beads and black smooth rudraksha earrings hung from nails on the wall. On seeing them, she realized that she was amidst hermits. Her eyes suddenly went to the trident smeared with vermillion. The light from the diya wavered in the wind, as did the little rag-like red and white flags. And right under the trident she could make out the shape of skulls.

Chandan shivered in fear. She almost lost her consciousness that she had regained with such difficulty. Was this the cave of a kapalik, some dreaded Shaivaite who meditates on corpses, or the ashram of a shamshan-saadhak, a Shaivaite who meditates in graveyards?

The snores of the sanyasini appeared to be striking some really high notes. Drenched in cold sweat, poor Chandan lay awake on her bed all night. She was not sure when she finally dozed off just before dawn. She had just fallen asleep when she felt a hand on her face. She opened her eyes without wanting to. A face as black as that of an African was moving towards her. On seeing the red, burning eyes in the black face, she might have let out a scream, but the laughter from the pearl-white teeth calmed her. This laughter proposed friendship.

'Are you hungry?' On hearing the mirth-laden question, her helpless body broke into sobs and shivers.

'Chhi, don't cry like this or you'll fall sick. Wait, I have just warmed some milk, just try to get in a few gulps somehow.'

The girl came back with a square bowl filled with milk, helped Chandan sit up and touched the bowl of milk to her dry lips. Chandan emptied the bowl in one go. Then that black girl helped her lie down again with great care.

'Just lie down quietly, understood?' She laughed and said, 'I'll come back after sweeping and mopping the temple. It will take some time because the temple is a bit far away.' She kept talking without even pausing to breathe. 'I'll come back with some bananas from the offerings for you. I am bolting the door from outside. Nobody is here today, the guru is out of town and Maya Didi has gone to her old akhada, she'll come back tomorrow. Hope her boat drowns.' She started laughing again.

'You haven't said a word, can you not speak?' This time, the black girl bit her lower lip. This restless girl was only wearing a thin sari that she had tied high. The glimpses of her vibrant youth through the sari's thin pleats made even Chandan, a woman, bashful. The wild child though had no time for bashfulness.

'Ok, new Bhairaviji, were you really unconscious day and night all these days?'

Chandan did not reply this time either.

'Hai Ram, are you really mute? Ram re Ram! He made you such a breathtaking beauty but didn't give you a voice. Praise the lord! Did you jump from the moving train because of this woe?'

Chandan kept looking at her strange, unfamiliar companion helplessly.

'Baap re baap! You surely don't lack courage! The very sight of that black-faced engine scares me. And do you know where you landed?'

She had heard that the sight of a snake bewitches birds. Just like that bird, Chandan was enthralled by the chatter of this wild girl.

'Just half a gajj away from a funeral pyre. Had you landed there even a few minutes earlier, then you would have become Ghoshal Babu's son's sati.' Wild Child finished talking and laughed loudly.

On seeing Chandan quite still, she continued her monologue, 'You are lucky that the guru was at the big cremation grounds in Shivpukur that day and was meditating under a tree. On seeing you coming flying down, the people who had come to attend Navendu Ghoshal's son's cremation ran away screaming "Ghost-Ghost", so the guru carried you on his shoulders and knocked on the door at midnight; it was I who opened the door. At first, I got scared. The guru had never brought a corpse home to meditate on, then why did he get one today? Then, after putting you in bed, he started screaming for Maya. That wretched Maya is lost to the world after a few drags of marijuana. When she failed to wake up, he told me, "Look Charan, had she fallen near the pyre on Amavas, it would have been a gift to the ashram. A burning pyre and virgin Apoorva's at that, who had died young. Even then, god has dropped this Bhairavi on us as an offering, in the middle of the cremation grounds and that too at the Shivpukur's grand cremation grounds, where there is always a pyre burning, be it day or night. You have to look after her, understood?" And I sat by your side all night. To be honest, I had started thinking that I was keeping watch on a corpse. The guru often prays through corpses; I thought maybe he was thinking of worshipping through the medium of this young girl, but when I kept my hand on your chest, I realized you weren't dead.'

'Is this a math?' Chandan asked in a low voice and the black girl hugged her. 'So, you are not mute. Why did you make me think you couldn't speak?'

'When did you give me the chance to utter a word?' Chandan laughed this time. She was speaking the truth. This talkative girl hadn't given her a chance to speak. 'What is your name?' Chandan spoke again.

'Charan, Charandasi. What's yours?' Her laugh lit up her dark face. The sweet smile on that large mouth travelled up her sharp nose and adorned her huge eyes as if with kohl.

'Chandan.'

'Matches with the colour of your skin. How are you so fair? Were your parents English?'

'Why?' Chandan started laughing. The simple question had distracted her from her backache.

'This one time, Maya Didi had gone to Naimisharanya to meet her old friends from her old akhada. One guard used to bring his mad daughter there to have ash put on her. She was light-skinned like you. That guard was Nikhalis Sahab, his wife was absolutely black and the daughter so fair that even a touch would blemish her. Ok, I should go. If Maya Didi came by, she'd get angry with me.' Tucking the end of her sari in her waist, she left.

Chandan was left alone. She wanted to pass out again. An unknown fear kept her in its grip. How could she run away, even if she wanted to? Dense forests all around, the large cremation ground in front of her with its arms wide open, an unknown place, strange companions! And then, how could she run away in her weakened state? She tried to stand with the support of the headboard. Her legs started shaking after a couple of steps. She sat on the bed panting, but was happy that her backbone was not broken. Had it been damaged, could she have taken even a step steadily? She stood up again. This time she walked to the door using the wall as a support. Confident, she walked back to the bed with steady steps. Her back still hurt but the bone didn't hurt like before. She would be able to regain her muscle strength by walking thus alone, she felt certain. On gathering this sweet fact, she lay down again, happy.

Her eyes went suddenly to a basket tied in a dark-coloured cloth. The lid of the basket seemed to be moving as if by magic. The lid fell off all of a sudden as if by an unseen force and the small knots of the cloth were pushed undone as a black shimmery snake emerged with its fangs out, making smacking noises.

Chandan sat coiled tight and trembling with fear. The snake started hissing and crawling about the room. Chandan couldn't help letting out a scream. A statue came and stood at the doorstep on hearing her.

'What's the matter?' She was shocked to hear the question posed in English. Ash smeared all over the body, shoulder-length hair in dreadlocks, some of which were golden and some grey, bloodshot eyes and the body naked.

'Why were you screaming?'

This time the question was answered by the hiss of the snake.

'Oh!' The serious countenance of the man dissolved into laughter at that. What a strange laugh, as if someone had dropped a boulder from the top of a tall mountain. 'Bhole's voice seems to have scared you.'

He walked in long strides to the basket. It appeared as if he had forgotten about Chandan's presence.

'Does my son need food? It seems that that greedy Charan has drunk his share of the milk again today.

The brass bowl isn't enough for my son. Isn't that what you are complaining about?' Chandan's heart was racing. It wasn't Charan who had drunk the milk in the brass bowl but her.

'Let Charan come back.' He was saying, 'Bite her dark body today and make it darker, ok?' Then, he picked up the snake from the basket and started rubbing it over his naked chest and stroking it as if it really were his beloved child. He coiled the mock-complaining snake around his neck and reassuring it lovingly and stroking it, went outside.

'I will feed my son sweet milk.'

Will that naked man feed his son and bring him back here to sleep? And what if he planted his bloodshot eyes and his long locks with his fierce visage in front of the helpless, prone Chandan's face? What would she do? The snake-charmer was no less fearsome than the snake. She hadn't been able to see his face properly. All she had seen were the bloody eyes and the ash-smeared chest. Had there been another door in the cave, she would have exerted all her willpower to run away. But if she takes the door he had taken, she would perhaps bump right into him.

He returned like a gust of unrelenting wind. In his hand was a bowl and around his neck, his darling son. He didn't look even look at Chandan once. As soon as the milk was finished, he kept down the smooth, thick body of the snake with such care, as if he were taking off a diamond necklace. When he had placed his precious jewel in the basket, Chandan saw something surprising, even dramatic. The man bent over the snake and the creature who had his head in the bowl lifted it up, touched its lips to his master's and then settled into the basket. This demonstration of love between man and his 'enemy' would remain the enduring image of that moment for Chandan. She kept staring at the sanyasi. The man tied the cloth around the basket and sat down cross-legged next to the trident. Then, he put the logs of wood lying around him in the shape of a triangle. He lit a stable fire and filled the room with smoke.

She could see the stranger more clearly when the window was opened. His whole body was smeared in ash, he was exceptionally tall and his upright posture even while sitting, made him seem like a statue covered in dust. He seemed unaware of his surroundings and didn't seem to be aware of Chandan's presence despite being in the same room as her. His solemn face and seriousness were like a light tearing into the room. Chandan kept staring at him. His face was so serene, no intensity, not even a hint of the anger he had felt at Charan mere moments ago. The ash-smeared calm eyes had long eyelashes, like a girl's. Even the eyelashes were coated with ash. Who was this mad yogi looking at? At his beloved snake, the cold ash or the skulls arranged like a pyramid near the trident?

His nakedness didn't worry Chandan. Every once in a while, he would toss the ashes a bit with his tongs and then smile like a child and look down. Chandan could make out he was laughing from the way his back shook. What was this memory that tickled him so? He struck the ashes with his tongs loudly and got up. The force of the tongs made the ashes scatter like fireworks in the entire room and the ash-filled smoke made Chandan gag. She closed her eyes. There was no knowing what this mad hermit would do next. When she opened her eyes, the smoke had pervaded the whole room and was making its way out of the door. From that curtain of smoke emerged Charan, walking towards her with a pooja thali in her hands.

'You are lucky that so many bananas were offered today.' Charan kept three or four bananas on Chandan's bed. Then she looked at the scattered ash and got scared, 'Hai Ram! Did the guru come back early today? It seems nobody came to the shamshan for a smoke today. And this black beast must have complained about me, haven't you?' Chandan understood what the girl was referring to.

'Why did you feed me his share of the milk, Charan?'

Charan put the plate next to Chandan and sat with a thump.

'Ok, so the guru is back and now that he is back, Maya Didi will also return soon. She can sense his comings and goings as if from the air. Then, would she let me sit next to you? Now tell me, did you jump off the train or did someone push you?'

A lump formed in Chandan's throat. She felt that she couldn't lie to this doe-eyed, simple, wild child. Before she could say anything, however, Maya Didi was at the doorstep rattling the beads of the trident.

'I knew it, knew it well.' Maya Didi's baritone rang across the entire cave. 'She'd be sitting with you and gossiping. Today is a Tuesday, the temple will be crowded. Did you go there or not?'

Charan kept sitting there unhappy and helpless. She didn't respond that she had returned from the temple a while ago.

'I have returned hungry and thirsty after having walked two miles,' Maya Didi started saying, 'but with this nincompoop around, I don't even have the pleasure of being asked whether I have had anything to eat or not. Which is why my sister gave me some snacks to eat when I was leaving. I said to her, "Didi, that black woman will not even ask me for water, it will be enough if she doesn't draw out all that I have eaten at your home".'

Then Maya Didi put the saffron bundle on her thick hips and took out thick chickpea rotis. Licking off the pickle kept between them, she wolfed down all the rotis one after another making Chandan feel like she was a merciless enemy sitting on her chest. She wanted to snatch the rotis from her. Perhaps the sanyasini too read the appeal in her eyes.

'What are you looking at? Do you want some? You seem very awake today.' Then, roaring with laughter, she handed a roti to Chandan almost as if she were reluctantly handing out alms. Chandan was so hungry that her self-esteem seemed to have disappeared like a cowardly friend. She leapt to snatch the roti.

'Looks like that greedy Charan didn't feed you.' Maya started saying, 'She will keep munching on something or the other given half a chance and if she is still hungry, she'll merrily run off to that Gopal's shop.'

After finishing all the rotis, Maya shook the cloth they had been wrapped in to collect the crumbs and ate them as well. Then, after emitting two long, powerful burp-notes, she called for Charan.

'Ai Charan, come here, can't you sit for a moment? Always running around. What are you chewing on now?'

Charan stood still like a statue, blowing her cheeks out. 'Listen,' saying so, Maya Didi stood up. On seeing her manly stature and structure, Chandan was a little surprised. Was she the same Vaishnavi she had found ugly in the dark of the night in her practically unconscious state? Had broad daylight worked some kind of magic on her? Calm and sharp eyes, a dusky but pretty face, like a rusty brass tumbler kept in a temple that had been scrubbed very thoroughly. Pouty, glistening paan-stained lips, a sharp chin adorned with a tattoo of three dots and a long bindi in a matching blue on her forehead that almost touched the parting of her hair and seemed to divide her glowing face into two halves. Right under it was the sandalwood teeka. Her voluptuous form had started sagging a little in places due to the ravages of age but the radiance of her face seemed to have rendered unheard the footsteps of time.

Her eyes were lined with a thick streak of kohl. The aroma of chewing tobacco wafted from her full mouth. Colourful beads in her rudraksha mala. Hair tied in a neat bun with a jimsonweed flower nestling in it. All these features were like oases cultivated with great care in the desert of her detachment. That face must have ensnared many men in its youth. Her large, shining eyes were the most prominent attraction. Anyone who gazed at them would find it difficult to look away.

'Careful!' Charan had later cautioned Chandan. 'Don't ever look into Maya Didi's eyes and agree to do anything. She has powers and can spear anyone just with her eyes.'

Honestly, Maya's personality was such. As if the spirit of the temples of sixty-four yoginis had come alive in her. Be it tantric powers, knowledge, science, religion or philosophy, she seemed to keep them all in her fists and attack Chandan with them every moment. Sometimes, those simple eyes would be filled with mirth, sometimes compassion, but the next moment, the calm face would turn stern. She would point her trident at Charan and stand like an angel of justice. Her eyes would fire such volleys that it seemed that poor Charan would turn to ash.

At such moments, her fire would only be quenched with the sudden appearance of the Swami. Like a magician, he would turn her into a lassie so quickly that Chandan would find it difficult to believe her eyes. Was she dreaming? Where had that old hag brimming with anger gone? This was the yogini's true appearance. Sometimes, a beautiful heroine and sometimes a mother-like Parvati. This must be the accomplished yogini's tantric victory. A true, simple, compassionate, sweet smile. She studied neither philosophy nor science. Worldliness was a mirage for her. The sky, virgin-worship, jagran, meditation, chakra-meditation—she had conquered them all but the greatest grief of her life lay like a stone on her chest making her sink a little more into the ground every day. The guru was a follower of the path of Siddha-amrit. The thirsty yogini could only admire that glass of golden nectar from a distance. Were she to even come close let alone touch, the Swami's aura would have burnt her. Chandan learnt this after a long time.

After ordering Charan to get a fresh chillum, Maya Didi sat down with her back resting against the wall. 'Wah! You have a remarkable face,' she said. 'But look, I like talking straight. This is the ashram of an Aghori sadhu. There are all sorts of followers coming here. Can we afford to pour ghee into such a raging fire?' Then Maya Didi's eyes glazed over as she was lost in thought.

'How can we keep such a beautiful Bhairavi here? I had been thinking of sending Charan to another akhada and now another problem has arrived.' Her voice suddenly rang out with annoyance. She was quiet for a moment and then started masticating the tobacco dregs in her mouth and said, 'Both of us keep wandering around the cremation grounds for knowledge.' Her face changed as soon as she mentioned the cremation grounds. The annoyed tone turned into soft, dulcet notes.

'I'll send you to my guru behen's akhada once you can start walking. If you want to get a letter or telegram sent somewhere that can be arranged too.'

Who would she call and how?

She had been thinking that she has been reborn in this narrow, dark cave. That she would start a brave new life as a hermit away from her relatives and acquaintances. But Maya Didi's instructions were clear. She had gained entry into the cave but she could not hope to live there. Will her mother who had run after her, wailing, the day she got married be able to embrace her if she found her alive? And like her mother, would she be able to contain her bubbling youth with self-control and be able to become part of genteel society? Suddenly, in that silent cave that was being swallowed by darkness, the shadows of three demons started roaming around her. The memory of poisonous kisses seemed to sting her like scorpion bites. She could not open that box of memories; she could not go back to her father's house or to her in-laws'. Be it an Aghori's akhada or any other akhada, the rudraksha mala that had landed around her neck was the only string she would hold on to and the guru's ash was now her vermillion.

Maya Didi didn't come back for a while and when she did, she took Charan with her. Chandan was now used to being alone. The day was at an end but they hadn't yet returned. Darkness had almost swallowed the cave but the smoke from the burning camphor in the room would keep finding its way into her mouth, making her feel as if she were being strangled. The potlis hanging from the beams swayed in the breeze like chandeliers. Breathing in the intoxicating fragrance of Mahua flowers wafting in through the window and listening to the tinkling of temple bells, Chandan forgot all her worries. Such was the joy in immersing the self in that unknown cell of devotion. Nobody here would find out who she was. Was she married or not? Why had she jumped off the train? What adversity had befallen her? As strange as this place might be, her companions were entirely devoid of curiosity and exuded calm. Even that talkative Charan had not repeated her audacious question and Maya Didi…? Mayavini! That strange devotee of Akhand Satchidananda! Could she stand even a sliver of emotion? Was there any place for sentimentalism in her? She did not want to know anything perhaps because she could divine things about people through her spiritual powers. Not just that, she could make the murderer in a cold case confess by cuffing him with her powers.

'A sin committed unknowingly is not a sin, Bhairavi!' Maya Didi had once said to a daydreaming Chandan, making her jump as if touched by hot iron.

How had Maya Didi found out about her? 'Had you sinned knowingly, that you had to jump? You are a fool, Bhairavi! Even a man made of stone would have forgiven all your sins on seeing that face of yours, and he was your lusty husband. He would have treated you like a queen. Anyway, now that the guru has put sacred ash on your forehead, it can never be adorned with vermillion.' Sighing deeply, Maya Didi left the room. Her voice seemed choked.

She had heard that the guru had put the sacred ash on her cold forehead when she was unconscious. He had put the rudraksha mala from the Shiv Mandir around her neck and stared at her for a long time.

'What will her name be after diksha, Guruji?' Maya Didi had asked. 'Bhairavi,' Guruji had answered and Maya Didi's face had turned purple. 'I really enjoyed it.' Charan said as she narrated the entire incident to her.

'Why?'

'You ask why? Have you ever seen your face in the mirror? Guruji put the mala around your neck with his own hands and gave you the name Bhairavi and then kept staring at you. All this made Maya Didi jealous. Have you not understood yet?' Now she was laughing. 'Or would she have left her house, three sons and husband at the age of 40 and chased him around cremation grounds?'

'Sometimes, she follows the guru around the cremation grounds the whole night. Sometimes, she meditates in the temple, sits like a stone, without eating or drinking anything, as if the life force had gone out of her body. I have to take the chillum there at such times. When I hand over the chillum to them, they almost seem like two corpses facing each other. Eyes as red as the embers of the chillum and that glowing face. How she changes! I start shivering and keep shivering even after returning home. Sometimes, they come out of meditation after three or four days.'

'If you feel so scared here, why don't you run away?' Chandan asked Charan one day. Charan turned to her like a wounded snake. 'When you can start walking, I'll ask you the same question, Bhairavi. We'll see what you say then.' And when Charan asked her that question exactly a month later, she did not have an answer.

TWO

It had been two months since she had come to this Aghori ashram. Maya Didi had probably forgotten her threat of sending her to another akhada. At night, Maya Didi made her sleep next to herself, with Charan at her feet. Sometimes, she'd wake up in the night to find them both missing from the bed. The first time, she had been so afraid that she couldn't even call out for them. What if someone attacked her from some dark corner of that dungeon? What would she be able to do? She remembered how once a large Kalpataru tree had been burnt to a stump by lightning, which was the reason she was frightened even of thunder.

Where could the two have gone? Had they abandoned her knowingly? Maybe they had an arrangement with that naked man? 'The guru had kept staring at you.' She had turned red with embarrassment when Charan had said that. He had put the mala around her neck with his own hands. She had only been wearing a sari and the touch of a man on her naked skin, just the thought was revolting. Sometimes, she would spend entire nights worrying. The two returned around dawn and lay down on the bed quietly but Maya Didi kept looking out of the window, god knows at whom. Her face would turn colours like a chameleon. The sun-kissed face with its large eyes, the Dhatura flower held fast in her high bun, her eyes lost in deep thought.

'So Maya Didi, will you get it?'

Charan spoke with Maya Didi only in Bangla. Anyway, even Maya Didi's Hindi sounded like it had been derived from Bangla. She was from the Chapra village in Bihar but her guru's first akhada had been in Burdwan. She would often call out to Bhairavi in that dialect, 'Latun Bhairavi', the new Bhairavi.

'Yes?' Maya Didi's reply reverberated like a roar in the cave, filling Chandan, who would be lying in a corner, with fear.

'Have you lost your mind? Do regular women have such eyes?' And that day Chandan would feel like she had hit the jackpot. Maya Didi would keep smoking chillums the whole day and be lost to this world.

That is exactly what happened that day, her night-long meditation reflected in her red eyes. Her chignon had come undone and her hair hung about her shoulders. The guru's camphor had been burning continuously but where was he? He hadn't even come to stroke his beloved. Charan might argue endlessly but she wouldn't even swallow a morsel without checking with Maya Didi. However, on seeing the latter deep in meditation, she was happily making garlic paste and polishing off stacks of rotis. She got a plate of rotis for Chandan too.

Maya Didi had trained her eye on a peepal tree, sitting quietly with an innocent smile on her face. Charan was taking advantage of this state of hers. First she drenched her rough hair with Didi's aromatic 'Laxmi Vilas' hair oil right in front of her and then took out mouth freshener from her saffron potli. Taking out kohl from her silver kohl box, she applied it to her large eyes and with a kohl bindi made her dark-skinned beauty even more luminous. Laughing, she sat next to Chandan.

'Why are you doing all this, Charan? Maya Didi can see everything.'

'So what, do you think she is still of this world? She'll stay this way till five or six in the evening. It is a lot of fun. Let me show you the temple today? Maya Didi will guard the house today, won't you Maya Didi?'

And that brat was on her knees in front of Didi asking. In reply, Maya Didi's wheat-hued face lit up with a smile.

Closing the door, she dragged Chandan out. She took her through maze-like, narrow alleys as if they were tied to a strong rope. Forest of gooseberries, greens of myrobalan, groves of tall coconut in places and in some places, calls of birds through hollow bamboo groves. Nature must have worked particularly hard to nurture the spectacle of greenery unfolding in front of Chandan's eyes. After they passed by a row of young saplings with blood-red buds, they saw bouquets of the Rangoon creeper arranged by Nature's own hands right in front of a decrepit mazaar. The aroma of the camphor burning at the mausoleum spread through the forest, rejuvenating it. With a lot of devotion, Charan swept the dried leaves off the mazaar with one end of her sari and then bent on her knees to pray.

'This is Chand Baba's mazaar. Every Friday, people from faraway places come here to tie threads and make wishes. They say that a thread tied here always bears fruit.'

And there really were innumerable, faded threads tied to the netted legs of the mausoleum.

'You see that yellow thread there? That's our Maya Didi's.' Charan started saying, 'I hid and watched her tying it one day. She was bawling her eyes out here. I know what she was wishing for.' She smiled mischievously, 'How can tying a thread help? The guru doesn't even look at her; after all I had tied that other red thread here.'

Chandan's head was spinning from having inhaled the aromatic camphor. Would she have to spend the rest of her life with these two women madly in love with their guru? 'Let's go, the temple is still far. Don't know if that Mad Gopal has also gone to the market. In that case, we won't even get one cup of tea.'

Chandan was also parched and she was bored of Tulsidas's Sattvik tea.

'Is he the priest?' She asked again.

'No.' Charan laughed and started walking faster, making Chandan huff and puff after her.

'That temple doesn't have a priest. He is the Chandal at the cremation ground and has a tea stall there. Sells a lot but that idiot can never keep his accounts straight. Had it been anyone else, they would have made thousands by now. I have told him often to keep some cakes or biscuits or some onion pakodas. After burning their dead, the tired gamblers on their way back home will eat some savouries and rest here. But he seems to have dung for a brain. Says, "Who'd eat onions after a cremation, what are you saying?" Now, who'd tell him? I have even seen a big brother uncorking a bottle under a Peepal tree after having cremated his younger brother. Here, everything goes. I have even seen a man who was cremating his wife being consoled with words like "Why are you feeling so sad? You are still so young. I have a beautiful niece of marriageable age." I wanted to push that uncle of the niece into that very pyre. Arre, at least let that wretched woman burn fully, you bastard! Who says these cremation grounds inspire devotion!'

'Do you come here often?' A surprised Chandan asked her, making Charan laugh.

'Yes, absolutely yes. Not just me, now you will also come here often. When Guruji comes here to meditate, I have to bring him his chillum. Then, Maya Didi would often say, "Just keep standing there, Charan. A virgin is at the centre of a guru's meditation. If you keep standing there, his meditation will bear fruit." Guruji just sits there as if made of stone. I hand over the chillum to him and watch these pageants from behind this very Peepal tree. When Mad Gopal spots me, he gets me the tea here. He might be empty in the head but his heart is of gold. He keeps clove, cardamom, cinnamon and other spices in a bottle. He says he makes special tea for me. But he is an absolute rascal otherwise, very wicked. Calls his stall 'Shamshan Vihar', a garden of funeral pyres it is indeed!'

Chandan was tired and out of breath.

'Ran out of breath so soon!' Charan wiped clean the top of a rock with the end of her sari and made her sit there even as she herself sat at her feet.

'I sometimes tease him mercilessly right in front of his customers. The tea is absolutely cold, you madman! Looks like you boiled it on the ashes of a cold pyre. He laughs and makes another cup. He wouldn't dare take offence at my words. He doesn't have the courage to look into Maya Didi's eyes though. Says, "The day your Maya Didi comes to burn here, I'll treat all my customers to complimentary tea." And there it is, his stall. Good that it's open.

'Oh you madman, where have you gone to?'

The coconut tree next to the stall shook and out of it, like a snake, with a body like a coconut, crawled the smiling madman and stood in front of them. He looked at Charan first and then at Chandan. His ugly pock-marked face lit up first with surprise, then joy and finally, curiosity covered it with creases.

A chill ran down Chandan's spine.

All she could see in front of her were the open cremation grounds, a steadily narrowing river and that giant Chandal. 'Wah wah! You found a splendid scarf today! Which beauty handed it over to you while climbing into the pyre? Give it to me, I'll wear it to the Vat-tala Mela away from that crone's eyes and look like a young bride, won't I?' exclaimed Charan.

She had draped that snatched-from-a-pyre scarf around herself and was admiring her reflection in the broken mirror in the stall. 'What are you doing?' A scared Gopal jumped in front of her as if hiding her. 'Can't you see! The owner's corpse hasn't even burnt entirely. What will the family say?'

But that mischief-monger of a girl had wrapped the scarf around her neck like a muffler and plonked herself on the broken iron chair in the stall.

'Let them see. It will be a while before they come back. Besides, they have their backs to us, they are not facing us. Haaye-haaye, she is so fair. From whose house is she? Just look at her feet, Bhairavi.'

Chandan glanced at the burning corpse with fear as if she were seeing one for the first time in her life.

Two fair alta-adorned feet had freed themselves from the constraints of the pyre as if the mistress of those young feet, not being able to stand the heat of the fire, was preparing to jump off it.

'She is Nand Babu's daughter.' Gopal started saying, 'She got married just last Phalgun. Don't you remember, I had fed you sandesh for her wedding? Came to her parents' home to deliver her child. Suffered for three days and died this morning.'

Charan took off the scarf in a tizzy. She still remembered the sweet taste of the wedding sandesh. How could she take the scarf off the corpse and fool around with it!

Chandan kept standing as if she were made of wood. She couldn't take her eyes off the burning pyre. When the flames started licking the young feet, she covered her face with her hands.

She had heard of a similar incident from her mother. Of the Upreti clan in the hills. The unborn child of such a child bride had taken her life. Had torn the womb asunder at the cremation grounds to come out, alive. He was called Upreti. She didn't know whether there was any truth in the account or if it was all make-believe; had the mistress of these fair feet also climbed the funeral pyre without having fulfilled her desire to see the face of her unborn child? The relatives standing around the pyre had backed away a little by now.

Was that her father—who had just last year with the fire as witness given her away for marriage—standing in the crowd here in the presence of the same treacherous fire to give her away yet again, with his head bent in helplessness?

'Oi Madman!' Charan's shrill voice surprised Chandan out of her reverie and she found the dark wraith-like madman staring at her. On hearing Charan's call, he moved to put the kettle on the fire. 'How that dratted man is staring at you! Looks like he is forgetting the charms of the old one after seeing the beautiful new Bhairavi. Isn't it so? Listen, by the time we come back from the temple, keep two cups of special tea ready. And if your relatives don't leave or if god forbid a new party doesn't arrive, get our tea sent to the back end.'

She brought Chandan to a narrow street.

Chandan found it all difficult to believe; on crossing paths with a funeral procession she used to wrap herself around her mother, and keep shaking and shivering with fear all night. But now, she was crossing the main cremation ground without a second thought. Sometimes the runaway flames of a pyre would stroke her sari; at other times the smoke of a dying pyre would make her nose and eyes sting: the kind of smoke that would come from their non-vegetarian neighbour's stove and enter her vegetarian mother's nose making her flare up in anger. 'May that meat eater die, looks like she is roasting lamb again, her son-in-law must be visiting.' Mother would say as she closed the windows and yawned.

Their neighbour was a Tibetan with four daughters and all four of her sons-in-law were sheep wool hawkers who often stopped to rest in their mother-in-law's house. It was in honour of these sons-in-law that she would roast sheep and consecrate the entire colony. The burning smell today reminded Chandan of her maiden home. She stopped walking for a moment. Charan reprimanded her again, 'Oh hello, walk fast, the temple is right there.' The thin flow of the river had formed a pool near the temple like the body of a young girl.

'Pull up your sari to your knees and hold my hand tightly, understood? Don't step on the rocks, they are very slippery; you'll be in bed again for a month if you slip off them.' The river was like a line around the temple, separating it from the rest of the world, and it was deep. The mischievous waves of the cold water began to pull her down and she got scared and lost her balance.

Somebody jumped up and held her. When she turned to see who it was, she closed her eyes in fear. Strange, strong hands held her up and made her stand and before the two could become alert, her saviour took a long jump and crossed the enormous flood made by the fountain. Even Charan who didn't think much of anyone was in shock for some time; then she laughed and pulled Chandan out of the deep end.

'Why did you get scared? That's what they do, come out of nowhere like snakes. The saying that a sanyasi and a snake live in the same house is true. Looks like they had been following us with their silken claws. They had surprised me too once.'

Chandan was unable to shake off the memory of those two long arms. Such warm hands, they were like embers of burning camphor. Had that creature been born from a volcano? Charan seemed to have read her mind. Had this restless young girl also gained enlightenment with her guru?

'What are you thinking, Bhairavi? You must have found the guru's hands very warm? The first time I was handing over the chillum to him, my elbow brushed against his and almost got a blister. Oh my god! Were they arms or logs on fire! You could cook roti on them.'

Then taking a long breath, she launched into a monologue, as if she were walking alone. 'He isn't a common man, like you and I. One camphor stick burns outside and one inside. Maya Didi also fires up in the same way sometimes. One day I had gone to Vat-tala to hand over the chillum and saw the two of them sitting across each other, like a snake couple. I heard the guru telling her, "The one Shiva calls Shakti, the entire creation sun-worshipping Maharajani, Boddh's Tara, Jain's Shri, Brahmagyani's Swadha, Vedic's Gayatri and the ignorant, Mohini, you are that Mahamaya, the great enlightened one." That day, Maya Didi's face glowed like never before. Long, black tresses, enormous eyes, sitting in Lalit asana, she was radiant like a goddess. She started saying, "You are my only Shiva, Guru and I am your Shiva Shakti."' Chandan listened, surprised by the wild child's erudition.

Had this unlettered girl picked up all this while cleaning and lighting chillums at this Aghori akhada?

Her long shapely legs were in the water one moment and out the next. Her faded sari dyed with palash flowers, adorned with a blue lotus and a border of large green leaves, fluttered in the wind, making it look like a Batik print quivering with sadness, a fettered aanchal; this butterfly flying around freely in the middle of nature's bounty, had she managed to memorize these things by listening to them every day?

'This is the temple. Wash your feet and walk behind me, you won't be able to walk without me guiding you.' She rang a huge bell tied with iron chains at the gate and went and stood at the stairs waiting for Chandan. The sound rang out like the fierce sound of church bells that echoed among the trees. To enter the ancient temple's doorway, Chandan had to contort her tall frame into an arrow. She lost her guide after taking a few steps into that fearsome darkness. 'Didn't I tell you to hold my hand!' Charan's voice was lost in supressed laughter and then she stood next to her flapping like a bat.

'Here, hold my hand and walk behind me.'

Stepping timidly on the floor, which was cold like a slab of ice, Chandan kept walking like a blind beggar holding Charan's hand. Almost half a gajj away, a tiny ghee lamp lit up a small room housing the linga, and it emitted a surprising amount of light.

Saying, 'Jai Shiva, Jai Guru' Charan started ringing the ancient silver bell hanging there. Chandan was caught unawares again. She could neither fold her hands in prayer nor could she blink her eyes. The temple looked so familiar but this was the first time she had set foot here! Was it a memory from a previous birth hidden in her subconscious? No, no, she had been assailed by the memory of walking into a similar blinding light after a great darkness in a different Shiva temple. Were all ancient Shiva temples deliberately built in the middle of such darkness? On that occasion, she had accompanied her mother to the Gyaneshwar temple while in ill-health. Her mother wanted to offer thanks for a wish-fulfilment. It was near a similar forbidding crematorium; she had had to step on an ice-cold floor, and a single ghee lamp lit up the linga there as well, the light falling across a brass idol celebrating the Chandravanshi king's taste in sculptures.

Mother's honeyed voice seemed to touch her eyelids now:

Trishradri Sankash Gaur-Gambheeram
Manobhoot Koti Prabhashri Shareeram
Sfoorannmoli Kallolini Charuganga
Lasat Bhaal Balendu Kanthe Bhujanga.

[The one who is fair-skinned like the Himalayas.
The one whose body glows like a thousand dignified gods of love.
The one from whose head the sacred Ganga flows.
The one whose head is graced by the small moon and from whose neck dangles a necklace of snakes.]

Who was singing the same paean to Shiva that was Ma's favourite? She looked around surprised and saw Charan swaying and singing while shaking the silver umbrella.

Mrigadheesh Charmambar Mundamalam.

[The one who wears a garland of skulls around his neck.]

This temple seemed to have been built by the kings of the Pala dynasty. The work of the Bengali sculptors in the form of the idols, their life-like expressions, folds of garments was unparalleled; the image of Parvati sculpted out of the black wall of the temple was riveting. To the south was the grand Shivalinga, with little Kartikeya stroking the lion-chariot on one side and on the other side was Ganesh on his mouse, dancing, with his trunk clutching his mother's sari. Fanning Parvati's head were the square leaves of the Kadali favoured by Bengali sculptors.

'The sacred fire here keeps burning all the time, it is our guru's. I come here every morning to light it. Come, I'll show you his prayer room!'

Charan and she crossed a bunch of spiral staircases to reach a room with a window with the kind of jaali work usually found in Imambaras. A river could be seen from the window. The air was refreshed by the breeze from the bamboo groves. From one nail hung a rudraksha mala and on another hung a black skull.

'Look, there's Gopal's shop! It almost seems like you can touch it from here but it must be about a mile away. Oh god, there are three pyres burning there! Has the entire Bashirghat village come to burn today? We won't be able to get a cup of tea on our way back either.'

Charan took out oil from a bottle kept there, made a cotton wick with great care and lit it. Then with folded hands, she stood in front of the rudraksha mala hanging from the nail. The lamp burning at the window threw out light from its many perforations. This jharokha that reminded Chandan of one of the handis of Garba dancers had two idols carved in them. One slim, tall and fair-skinned and the other shiny dark-skinned, plump, striking a dancing pose like a Nepali khukri, and symbolising Vankanya who changed her form like nature.

'Let's go!' She touched one rudraksha bead to her dark forehead and turned around. 'Let me put a log in the fire and then we can go back.' Charan took her on another long pilgrimage, finally arriving in an entirely different room where wood was stacked up like a pillar. Charan pulled out a thick log from the pile. She sensed Chandan's curiosity again. 'You must be wondering who could've dumped all this wood in the midst of this wilderness. A huge fair happens here on Shivratri. Both Hindus and Muslims are followers of Shiva. I have heard that in the Sunderban jungles, labourers still meditate taking the name of our guru's guru. Even tigers feel frightened on hearing his name. The only offerings accepted here are Dhatura flowers and wood for the sacred fire. That is all our Shiva asks for! This one time, a merchant from Kolkata arrived here and offered ten trucks full of wood.' Charan wiped her hands after putting the thick log in the fire. Then she started opening the knot in her pallu.

'Let's rest for a bit and then leave. Earlier, I used to return only in the evenings. One puff and then only sleep. I have come prepared, don't worry.'

She took out a small chillum from the knot of her sari and then reaching out behind the idol took out a small packet and poured its contents into the chillum and started laughing, 'I take one prasad of Shiva here and one at home. The one I take here staves off the fear of ghosts and spirits on the road, and the one at home, of the witch there. Ever since the shakti mandal here was pulled away by a lion, I have had to run back sooner.'

Lighting the full chillum with the sacred fire, she roared, 'Jai Shiva Guru' and touched it to the Shivalinga and then to her forehead. Then, cupping the chillum with both her hands, she took a long drag and started coughing. The light of the lamp was waning. Charan was acting like she had had an attack of madness.

She was dancing, coughing and singing, 'Jai Bum, Jai Bum, Bumlahari, Bum Bubum Bubum Bum Bumlahari.' Her voice echoed through the temple.

What could Chandan do?

On the one hand were the roads lost in the smoke of burning pyres, the chance of running into ravenous and cunning lions, the walk through long and winding roads, the aggression of the Chandal, the memory of eyes that could look into your very soul; on the other, in a dark, strange temple a companion lost in the intoxication of marijuana.

What if two ash-smeared arms embraced her?

Chandan tried to snatch the chillum away before the lamp went out. 'What are you doing, Charan, don't smoke any more. Let's go home, I am scared.'

She choked as she said that. Her outstretched arms caught at nothing and kept hanging in the emptiness. Two burning, intoxicated eyes carved into the Shiva idol on the temple's broken walls seemed to be shooting arrows at her, pushing her back. Where did that idol come from? Was this tantric temple making her see things or was the smoke from Charan's magical chillum getting into her nostrils and making her hallucinate!

'It isn't just marijuana.' Charan bellowed with laughter. 'There's something else in it too—the poison of dog piss! Understood? One drag and you are a queen! Pluck diamonds off golden trees and eat them. That's the reason Gopal says, "A girl is better than the boy who hasn't smoked weed."'

It was such a fearsome idol! Parvati on her lion and Ganga on her tortoise. On one end, Nagalok carved in stone, half the body human and the other half serpent. Shiva's descendants with their hands folded, with feet in motion as if the whole temple would ring out with the sound of their footsteps—khat khat khat! Above them heaven, different gods on different chariots, in the middle, Shiva dancing with his ten hands, and around his neck, the snake! Chandan took a few steps back just on seeing it. This looked like the beloved snake of that sanyasi. The lamp had gone out. All Chandan could see were Charan's red eyes and the embers of her chillum.

'Jai Guru, Jai Guru! Here, you also take a drag, then we can leave.' Charan invited her but Chandan kept standing still.

'Don't say no, it is Shiva's prasad. Here, this is how you take a drag.' Shrinking her nose, she took a long drag. After this presentation, she took Chandan's hand and made her sit next to her with great affection. She put the chillum on Chandan's trembling lips.

'Take it, take a drag. Are you deaf? Can't you see it has gotten dark?' Charan reprimanded her.

Chandan wasn't sure if it was because of the smoke that had entered her nostrils or the censure in Charan's eyes that she found herself taking a drag.

She coughed and then it was like somebody had taken her flying. She was walking behind Charan like a sleepwalker. The muscles that had tied themselves into knots due to a long spell of lack of nutrition were unknotting on their own with alacrity. Chandan kept walking on, spearing the great darkness of that wilderness. She walked on that unknown water body where she had earlier trembled and lost her footing with such confidence, it was as if it was the familiar pool in front of her house.

Charan kept gabbing the whole way but Chandan did not hear her in spite of her attempts to do so. Her soul seemed to be wandering. This time, Charan had taken some other route to the ashram. Maya was still in the condition they had left her in.

'Didn't I tell you?' Charan started saying, 'She'll keep swaying like a madwoman for another day or two—I had crushed fresh marijuana and put it in her chillum. Hello? Have you lost your mind to one drag? We still have to take one drag at home. Didn't I tell you, one drag to stave off the fear of ghosts and spirits on the road and one to chase away the fear of the witch at home? Let me prepare it now, then take a drag and forget all your woes. Right?'

Chandan looked at her with her eyes glazed over.

'Oh my god—you look like Yogamaya! Your eyes look so sleepy. Let me give you one more drag before you sleep so that being somewhat intoxicated doesn't bother you. Just take this puff and get into bed and then you can meet all the people you wanted to meet in your dreams.' Charan laughed and left to return with a replenished chillum.

She took Maya Didi's hands and put her in bed like she was a child but Didi got up as soon as she had lain down and started creating a scene. Pulling her saffron sari to her knees, she started clapping. She laughed sometimes, then cocking an eye at Chandan started singing in Bengali:

> Mann na rangaye,
> Kaapad rangale
> Ki bhool korile jogi.
>
> [You didn't colour your heart but only your clothes.
> What a fault you committed oh, jogi!]

Maya Didi's singing voice was deep like an old courtesan's. And even if she couldn't understand the meaning of the words, Didi's gestures explained to Chandan the gist of the song. Who would say she was a bhairavi? What kind of an intoxication had made her fall so?

Was it the smoke of the chillum or the smoke of nature's chillum? What were these unfulfilled desires that this bhairavi was brimming with?

'Let it be, Maya Didi. You don't have to do more drama!' Charan's scolding made Maya Didi pause. Charan made her lie in bed and pulled her blanket up to her face.

'No Charan, my darling, beloved Charan! Just give me one more drag.' Maya Didi started begging and Charan, laughing, pulled the chillum out of her reach this way and that, teasing her like a master does with his dog.

'Ok, here take only one drag. I have to take one, then there's the new bhairavi.' Maya Didi uttered a child-like laugh, took a long greedy drag and fell into a deep sleep as if she were unconscious.

Then, that chillum took Chandan from the here and now to a dream land where she met all the people she had lost in the last few months. Her memories sometimes took her to Dharchula, sometimes to Delhi and sometimes to Shahjahanpur. Her aunt was laughing at her…

THREE

'Good! I had told you to not to climb your mother's funeral pyre but that's exactly what you did, girl.'

This aunt had made her cry so much three days before the wedding. She had not slept all night. Why had Mother invited this damned aunt! But what could Mother have done? The aunt was after all the wife of her father's brother, how could she not have been invited. Though her mother had been smart and had written such a clever letter that even if she had taken a plane, her aunt wouldn't have reached on time. God knows, how she found out in time.

'It doesn't matter that you didn't invite us!' She taunted mother a lot, wiped her crocodile tears and thick stubby nose with the corner of her sari. 'Blood is thicker than water—I took a loan from wherever I could and came running as soon as I got the news.'

On the third day when mother left for the market, Chachi dragged her to the terrace, 'Do you think I am lying?' She squinted her cat-like eyes, making them shine like marbles, and continued, 'I wouldn't have said anything to you but then I thought that she is going to another house and that too a house so affluent that neither you nor I can even think of touching the dirt of their shoes. The reputation of this house is now your responsibility, my child. Don't climb your mother's pyre, girl.'

And that's how she started telling her the story of how her mother's reputation was besmirched. Chachi kept on with a deluge of tears: at times for Chandan's dead father, and at other times, while talking about the profound grief of Chandan's Nana.

'It was the generosity of my Jethji that he salvaged the reputation of a Brahmin girl, otherwise nobody swallows a fly voluntarily. Your poor Nana! I heard that he jumped into an abyss and killed himself. Your Nani also took her own life. They couldn't show their faces in society because of your mother's ill repute.'

Chandan cried all night. The calm face of her serene and simple mother kept smiling at her. No, her mother could never be like that. This was certainly the frustrations of the envious Chachi bubbling over. She was cooking up stories to torture her niece. Chachi was dependent on her Jeth and Jethani despite being married. Chandan's jobless Chacha had stayed a slave to his Tau. He was either dropping Tau's children at school, or going grocery shopping, or taking his brother's family to the hills and at times, house-sitting in their absence. On the other hand, her mother was independent despite being a widow. She had embraced widowhood and overcome it. She had defeated it. Having become a school principal after completing her MA and MT, she and her daughter lived in a government house. Over a dozen teachers trembled at her name night and day. She had servants and peons. She had a beautiful and calm daughter who had received a proposal from such an affluent and handsome young man and was going to live like a queen in his house.

Why wouldn't Chachi burn in envy? Nobody had wanted to marry her dusky daughter despite her mother's thousand attempts. She even got her daughter admitted in a medical college. The daughter made such academic progress, however, that she eloped with a nincompoop classmate of a different caste! Perhaps the realization that no one from their community would ever come to her house for a wedding was like a sucker punch for her and it was the pain of that blow that made her spew this bile.

There was some substance to Chachi's accusations though. It was her mother's beauty that had made Nana give her the name Rajrajeshwari. From head to toe, this Rajrajeshwari had the luminescence of Nanda Devi being carried in a palanquin to be submerged in the river.

Nani's maiden home was in Nainital's New Bazar. Nani had gone there for her delivery. Maybe it was the fair beauty of the daughter of the Shah family prancing about on their terrace next door that had touched the daughter in her womb. Like all Shah women, that girl too had a milky complexion, sharp nose and such a glowing, smooth forehead that it seemed like it would bleed at the slightest touch. Such beauty, and to top the calamity, at fourteen she looked like she was twenty-four! The Shah girl seemed to have been blessed with beauty and health in equal measure.

Nani was Nana's third wife and an only child, so her father had raised her like a son. He had wanted to get her the best education and husband and house. It was this stubbornness that made him send his daughter to the Missionary School in Almora against all opposition from his family. He moved to Dharchula to conduct his trade in woollen and silk carpets and bought a house in Almora for his wife and daughter so that his daughter would not lack for anything. By the time she was in high school, Rajrajeshwari had mixed her convent education with the glow of beauty and increased her value manifold. Now, she could marry into any good family and add to the family's prestige. That was when it all went wrong. The queen of temptation was lured into the land of longing.

Rajrajeshwari had a friend in school who was more beautiful than her. The day this classmate had visited their house for the first time, she had surprised everyone with her loveliness, including Rajrajeshwari's mother.

'Aha! Whose daughter is your friend?' She had asked her daughter as soon as the friend left.

Rajeshwari was a little rattled but gave her the details. Her mother was enraged, 'Look at the audacity of that Paturia girl! You dare not be seen in her company ever again. I had told your father that you are sending your daughter to a Christian school, she will be sitting with girls from all castes there. But he doesn't listen to anyone. Started sermonizing me instead saying "everyone is equal in God's eyes, Raji's mother"! But you listen to me, girl.' Mother shook Rajeshwari's shoulders and said, 'I'll bury you alive if you continue fraternizing with her. That low caste girl with the airs of a princess!'

Her warnings were like a drizzle in the wilderness. All that happened was that Rajeshwari's friend Chandrika never visited them at home again. Rajeshwari kept visiting her at her own home on the sly. Chandrika's mother received Rajeshwari in her home with as much love as the disrespect Rajeshwari's mother had shown in closing her doors to Chandrika. It was true that Chandrika's mother was a winsome warrior, and an eyesore for all the mothers of daughters in Kumaon. In those days, a rich man who didn't have a few mistresses with such unparalleled beauty was considered wretched. In those days, having mistresses was a status symbol. If a rich man didn't have a mistress, it was thought that he was facing the prospect of penury.

For a long time, the sight of such a beautiful flower had made even Chandan's Nana buzz around her like a greedy bee. The attentions of that renowned man

[Chandan's Nana] had made Chandrika's mother lose interest in her work. A lot of musical instruments had fallen lifeless of their own accord in that time. The musicians had left for other patrons on not being paid. Anklets had collected dust. The white membranes of the dholak had turned black with disuse, like kohl-lined eyes with cataract. It was only the love of the beautiful third wife that had brought Chandan's Nana back home. He didn't go back to that basti even by mistake after that marriage.

The courtesan also got married to someone she liked and set up home. The man for whom she left all her wealth and her trade, gave her everything. A large house to live in, a son and a daughter. Both equally good-looking. The son was studying in the Army School and the daughter in the local convent.

'Ma, Miss Summerville says that she will send me abroad on behalf of the school. You get Bhaiya married by then and make yourself free of responsibilities. I'll get a job and you can come and live with me in peace,' a chirpy Chandrika would say, making her mother laugh. Whit of a girl but such wisdom!

There was no peace to be had here. Will society let her erase the stigma of her past life? Or would she only be able to start life afresh across the seven seas?

Her children's father was not an ordinary man. Chandrika had the blood of Kumaon's royalty in her veins. It was for this reason that when Chandrika turned adamant about something, her mother felt great pride. The stubbornness of royalty, of women, of children! She was always willing to bear all her daughter's whims.

Rajrajeshwari was caught unawares when she first saw the opulence of her friend's family. The furniture boasted intricate handwork; there were grand mirrors, chandeliers and Tibetan carpets. When Chandrika's mother walked in with snacks on a silver plate, the young girl didn't see her at first. Her eyes were riveted to a portrait painted in oils on the wall. Fitted Nepali pyjamas, bandgala coat, sequinned silk cap and a moustache as bushy as the tail of a Tibetan sheep. A thin, silver watch on the wrist, and shiny loafers on the silk carpet gleaming like they had just been scrubbed clean.

'What are you looking at, child?' Chandrika's mother asked with a smile in her voice, making Rajrajeshwari snap out of her reverie.

'That's your friend's father. Whoever comes here, looks at that painting first.'

Now, it was the sight of the living mother and not the dead father that engrossed Rajeshwari. As tall and as strong boned. Even at this age, her figure could give a young girl a run for her money. It was the face that bore the marks of the ravages of time and misfortune. 'Whose house have you lit up, girl? Who is your father?' The voice of the professional singer rang out like the peal of anklets.

'Mahimchandra Tiwari of Vishad is my father.' Rajeshwari gave this bit of information in an even tone but on receiving it the face of that impressive hostess paled in grief. She regained control the next moment, however, and said, 'Nice, then you come from a family known to us. Where is your father these days?' She pulled the chair close to her and sat down.

'Do you know my father?' Rajrajeshwari asked and then went quiet when she remembered her mother's angry words. I hope she doesn't find our address and arrive at home, she thought.

'Why wouldn't I know him, who doesn't know Tiwariji? No Holi festivities are complete without him.'

Rampyari was speaking the truth. The overflowing jug of thandai, plates full of pahadi gujiya and bits of potatoes being sent by Rajeshwari's mother to the drawing room during Holi. The latter would sometimes get hassled and angry but the next moment, Mahimchandra's sugar-sweet voice would ring out in song making even Rajeshwari feel shy; her mother would hide behind the curtains and sway [to the beat].

Father's fair face would turn red with the effort of perfecting the high notes. With one palm on his ear, he would make the gathering echo with the Pahadi Chanchar Taal, a folksy drum-based rhythm of Uttarakhand:

'Jaye padoon pee ke ank
Chahe Kalank Lage ri!'

[I'll embrace my lover even if it gives me a bad reputation.]

The timbre of the gathering would rise to reach the high notes of 'Ank' as if it were a ball thrown in the air.

Reminiscing about the same things, Rampyari asked again, 'Where is Tiwariji these days?'

'Dharchula!'

'Oh god! So far. What he is doing there?'

'He trades in shawls, rolls of wool and carpets.'

Rampyari was sad all of a sudden. Oh god, how far had that knowledgeable admirer of beauty fallen! The trader of the market of beauty had in the end become the trader of smelly Tibetan shawls, rolls of wool and carpets! She looked at Rajrajeshwari again.

She had been so foolish!

Why hadn't she been able to recognize her lover's daughter at first glance? The girl's features were exactly like his and that slight stammer in the voice was the same too!

And here she was thinking of asking for the girl's hand for her handsome son. Now, even the thought of such a match was a sin. Her thoughts and plans were immaterial. Has anyone been able to change the Almighty's plans? Has he ever failed to carry them out?

Rajrajeshwari started visiting her friend at home on the sly after school every day. With time, the friend's brother became dearer than the friend. The Greek god had come home for holidays. They would play cards or go on picnics. Rampyari would watch them helplessly from the window and a bitter smile would mar her face. They roamed about in the neighbourhood, a circumscribed territory. Sometimes, they'd go around the big house on walks and on these occasions, the beautiful and intelligent sister would stay behind knowingly while the two lovers would sit and chat, with their feet in the cold water of the neighbourhood pond. There was no question of going further out; Almora was a tiny town and old people who had romped about in their youth would walk around with their eyes trained on youngsters.

Rampyari was aware of this, and yet chose to let them be. What was the harm if her son got a high-born Brahmin girl? A daughter-in-law like Rajrajeshwari would be as precious to her as a plate of sesame. And that Brahmin would also be taught a lesson, the one who had kicked her glorious loveliness away on seeing the beautiful face of his wife.

The young couple had made all the foolish designs of youth. Kundan planned to get a job in a year. Just for that one year, Rajeshwari would have to deal with the labyrinth of her father's sternness. But one day, feeling lost in that labyrinth, struggling with it, she escaped into Kundan's arms. She enveloped her young lover in her soft body near that very neighbourhood pond. Her father didn't just fix her wedding but her wedding date too. It was a mystery how he had found out about his daughter's romance. The daughter of a Kumaon Brahmin marrying a Kshatriya, and the son of his former mistress at that, he would kill his only daughter without a second thought before that could happen! But even that street-smart man made a mistake. Rajrajeshwari jumped from a tall window like a wild cat and ran into her lover's arms.

The young man was neither experienced in the ways of the world nor did he have the time to think things through. The rest of the story was one of grief and grief alone. Rajrajeshwari's father caught up with the fleeing lovers at the Laal Kuan station. So overwhelmed with rage was he that he would have shot Kundan on the spot, but the latter slipped away like a Japanese Jujitsu master and hid under a pile of sugarcane on a goods train. The heartless Tiwariji dragged the trembling Rajrajeshwari home from love's golden lair by her hair. She was taken out of school and locked up at home.

Tiwariji spent thousands of rupees to ensure nobody found out about his daughter's sullied reputation, but these things never remain hidden. Even a murmur of such a love story rolls off the hills and turns into a folk song sung at fairs and uttered by a thousand mouths. When the story of his daughter's shame started being narrated, Rajrajeshwari was hidden behind stronger doors. As time passed, this song of shame started echoing across the wide hills.

'Aha, kundani rangrootha
Meri Raji ke nhilego!
Meri Rajula bhali Baana-
Meri Raji nhilego!'

[The handsome Kundan has taken my Raji away!
My beautiful Rajula was taken away by my Kundan.]

These four lines and her foolish actions seemed to have thwarted the fortunes of Chandan's mother. Nobody from the hills would be able to forgive the stupid girl who had run away with the son of a prostitute. In the eyes of the simple hill clans, it was a grave sin that could not be forgiven. Who would believe that Tiwariji's daughter was unsullied? Which trial by fire would help reinstate her in society?

Mahim Tiwari had even prostrated himself before his poor friends and pleaded with them. Perhaps, the son of one such friend who had only studied till Inter could be bought with the promise of wealth. A year ago, Tiwariji would not have even bothered to spit in that boy's direction, but now he found that it was his friend spitting at him instead.

'No, Mahim!' The friend put his hands in the pockets of his torn coat, stood ramrod straight and said, 'Though poor, even we have a reputation to think of. We might be hungry but we will not eat the leftovers of a feast.'

That very night Tiwariji stepped out to find a groom for his daughter like a wounded snake, after shaking up the whole house with his anger. He was ready to marry off his feckless daughter to whomever he could find, be it a blind man or a man without arms or legs. He would wash his hands of that girl who had turned out to be a blot on his family name. He got more than he had expected. He found a rich man from the same caste as a son-in-law. In the fear that the extended family would turn the groom away by telling him everything, he took his daughter and wife away from Almora to Haldwani for the wedding.

'Organizing a wedding in the hills in January is no child's play!' He cleverly circumvented the questions about his departure. 'That is the reason I am spending so much money to go to Haldwani.'

But people cottoned on. Some of them even said biting things to the wounded lion, 'Oh Mahim, we hear you are even taking Rani Rampyari for the kanyadaan!' Some of his so-called friends even laughed at that; after all, since the time Rampyari had married the king, she had acquired the title of queen without even wanting it. Mahim swallowed the bitter pill and hung his head in shame. What could he do? Had the cursed girl not even left him a pail of water to drown himself in?

The groom was a childless widower who owned a huge sweetmeat shop in Shahjahanpur. Many years ago, he had run away from home and started a stall that sold gajak and rewri. In those days it would have been difficult to buy a mere bowl of oil. With Lakshmi's blessings he now had two dozen servants playing about at the shop. Rajrajeshwari's mother started wailing at the sight of the groom. A receding hairline, gap-toothed and to top it, a face that had turned black working in front of a roaring fire. Rajrajeshwari's wedding seemed like a funeral. The sight of his wife's tear-filled eyes perturbed Mahim Tiwari no end. He started staying away for business. One day, his troupe of yaks and sheep came back without its leader. Search parties found his dead body in a cavern after many days of looking. Perhaps an angry yak had pushed him off the hill or maybe the emptiness in his life had made him plunge into the abyss to scatter himself away.

Within just a few days, Rajrajeshwari discerned from the behaviour of her fifty-year-old husband that news of her exploits had reached him despite her father's many attempts to keep things from him. This made her careful and take every step with caution. She never laughed or dressed up or applied make-up. She didn't even go to the veranda or the terrace, leave alone stepping outside the house. She never stood before the mirror. For his part, the jealous husband thought it prudent to fortify his fortress. He locked his wife in when he left for the shop. Chandan was born exactly a year later but her mother remained locked in. He could not accept with equanimity the daughter borne honestly by his beautiful wife. His ego had probably twisted his mind to a certain degree. The shop was being run by servants now. He kept buzzing around his imprisoned wife like a bee all the time. He kept asking her the same question, 'Is she really my child? You haven't diluted the milk, have you?'

He would then frighten her with his demonic laughter only to calm down the next minute.

'Have you gone mad?' She would smile with such sweetness that he'd be reminded of the sugar syrup in his shop.

'So, you haven't been touched even by air?' He would walk around her, turn her around like a betel leaf and say, 'Don't be offended but I read in the papers the other day that some woman in a foreign land gave birth in the thirteenth month. Given a chance, I would shoot the journalist reporting such news. What do they get from messing with the happiness and peace of a household!'

Rajeshwari's skin would crawl with revulsion. She would feel like drowning her short, toothless black man in his own sugar syrup, but tolerating all this also felt like repentance to her. The more the suspicious man tried to oppress her, the more she would get oppressed. To distract herself, she would keep herself busy with fasts and ceremonies. She had become the better half of her old husband in the true sense of the word. He would keep testing her fidelity at every step and she would never let herself fail. At times, he would spit in the plate while coughing and then push it towards his wife, saying, 'Eat from this plate, you have served too much vegetable. Why do you cook so much?' And she would quietly suffer the punishment for having cooked too much by swallowing the leftovers from his plate like a meek cow.

FOUR

Chandan was not even two when Rajrajeshwari became a widow. When the old man died after suffering from a fever for five days, he had not even told her where he had buried all his wealth. What happens to inheritances is what happened in this case too. Because of an unwritten will, all Rajrajeshwari got was a big haveli, a blind and deaf 80-year-old mother-in-law, seven or eight cooking utensils and eight to ten plates of stale laddoos and barfis, which were eaten by whoever could get their hands on them.

Her husband's older brother was a tobacco merchant in Kutch; how could he drag the blind mother to that distant land? The younger brothers and their wives had backed out of taking her responsibility even earlier. That is how, poor Rajrajeshwari ended up living in that palatial haveli with her child and old mother-in-law. The only happiness she had experienced after getting married was that of living in a haveli. Attired in his worn-out vest and dhoti, her miserly husband had flung all desires into the oven that was his livelihood. It was a mystery how the same man had displayed such generosity in building such a splendid haveli.

The wise Rajrajeshwari mapped out her plans for the future as soon as her relatives took her leave after her husband's tehraveen. How was she going to live in such a large house with her infant, and an elderly, blind and deaf mother-in-law who was more of an infant? She retained three rooms for her own use and donated the rest of the house to a girls' school. The news of the young widow's generosity spread through the town. Some said, 'How generous of her. She could have let out the house to an office and lived off the rent for the rest of her life without even lifting a finger.' Still others said, 'Just wait and watch! That miserly old man will climb up the chest of the principal of the girls' school and take her life.'

Nothing of the sort happened. The school started running and became a college and with that college progressed the courageous Rajrajeshwari. The school's principal was the old Mrs Khanna. She had herself suffered at the hands of child marriage. The cracks in her feet had made her feel the misery of other people. She had revolted against widowhood and left it far behind. She taught all the skills of dealing with a lonely heart and a raging society to her young and talented protégé and then dragged her straight to the ring. Rajrajeshwari started studying under her loving guidance. The childless Sharda Khanna took Chandan into her loving embrace. Chandan addressed her as Dadi and called her own dadi, Hauva.

Chandan's Dadi had indeed become a hauva by then. Sometimes, she would undo her bun and spread her tangled white hair all over her face. She'd howl out her dead son's name and at times, at times she'd create such a vulgar display of her unsatisfied youth's boisterous memories that all the ruffians on the road would clap their hands and egg her on with the crassest of words. One night, she left the house in such a state, crying and wailing, and never came back.

After having put Rajrajeshwari on her feet, Sharda Khanna also took voluntary retirement a few years before her time and went to live with her sister abroad. She had really wanted to take Chandan with her but that canny woman knew that Rajrajeshwari lived for her only child. She did not insist on taking Chandan with her. She did not want Rajrajeshwari to think that she was being asked for a fee for what she had done selflessly. The benevolent Mrs Khanna made sure of that. Mrs Khanna embraced Chandan who had become dearer to her than life, dried her tears and dragged Rajrajeshwari to a quiet corner of the aerodrome.

'Rajeshwari!' On her way out, she whispered her gurumantra into the ears of her friend and protégé, 'Get the girl married at the earliest. Don't give her too much freedom, understood?'

'Why?' Rajrajeshwari's heart started sinking.

After all, she always kept her eyes clapped on her beautiful daughter. She was determined that her daughter would not suffer the same fate as hers at the hands of youth. Each day, she went with her daughter when the latter went to college and came back with her. She kept circling her daughter like a vigilant lioness. But hadn't she cheated her similarly vigilant mother in her time? Amma had never been able to guess anything, then how would she? Perhaps, Sharda Behenji suspected something.

'Don't be silly!' Sharda caught hold of her lithe wrists, 'For you, your Chandan is still the one without a frock, panty-clad child running around, isn't it? You will not find a prettier girl in the entire city even if one were to set out to search with a lamp, Rajeshwari! Such beauty that even old women like me forget to blink our eyes, then how can any young man remain unmoved? Just look at your neighbours for example. That house is filled with strapping, young men. Had they been of your caste, I would not have worried. You could have organized a swayamvar of a thousand princes in your courtyard with just a flick of a finger. But I pray that none of them clap their eyes on Chandan. Which is why I am telling you, Rajeshwari, you have accumulated a lot of leave; take a long holiday, go to the hills, find a good house there and get this done with. Finding a groom for a beautiful girl is not a problem in any society. Such lucky mothers do not need to look for grooms. The grooms find them.'

Sharda Behenji had spoken the truth.

Drowning in anxiety, roaming in the veranda, Rajrajeshwari kept looking at the havelis around hers. The tall houses of the wealthy Rohilla Pathans of Saharanpur surrounded her haveli as if resting their hands on its shoulders. The fair, blue-eyed sprite-like maidens [of those havelis] would invite beautiful Chandan over every day. It would be one festival or the other and she'd have to go with Chandan for every one of them. Before Rajrajeshwari could say yes or no, sometimes Tahira whom Chandan had known since childhood would drag her away or sometimes Naseem! She did not know when their Eid would become her daughter's Eid! The thought started bothering her. At the end of the day, when Chandan would return from her friends' celebrations, decked in khus and henna, Rajeshwari would scrutinize her so closely that she would see the very marrow of her innocent face. She hadn't noticed Chandan's beauty till now. Had Sharda Behenji's wisdom changed Chandan in one day?

Such fair skin and incomparable eyes, the latter highlighted by the kohl that Tahira had applied in them, and that dupatta, in the deep green favoured by Muslims, made her fair skin even more prominent.

'Aunty insisted on making me wear all these bangles, Amma! They are worth four rupees.' She would stress on 'aunty's' generosity, trying to soothe her mother's frayed temper. She knew that though her mother did not say anything, she could reprimand with her eyes in such a way that it would seem like corporal punishment.

All the boys in the Muslim neighbourhood were also one handsomer than the other. One was studying at Pakistan's Engineering college and had come here to spend his vacation and another was training to be a doctor in Aligarh; they would all whistle and roam around the house. The minute she'd hear of any of them coming home for vacations, Rajeshwari would start following her daughter everywhere like the Gestapo. She was familiar with every warren of the city of love. She could sniff out when and how her daughter might bamboozle her. However, she had sensed no deception or betrayal on the part of her innocent daughter so far, but any moment could turn into dynamite and detonate her household. Then why shouldn't she, who had been burned herself, take precautions in time?

Before this, she hadn't taken even ten days off her long, boring job, but the very next month, she applied for two months' leave on the pretext that a letter had arrived from home. It appeared the house that her parents had lovingly built was falling into ruin, and she had to take care of it.

There was no end to her daughter's excitement on their journey but as they started approaching Almora, her mother's mood began to turn uncharacteristically sombre. As soon as they reached the Lal Kuan station, Rajeshwari was filled with terror. She suddenly felt like she would once again have to face her father's violent rage. That her lover, shivering in the foggy winter, would have turned into a white statue, waiting under a lamp post for her.

She had not informed her relatives about her arrival in Almora. Instead she had sent a telegram to one of her dear fellow principals, who was now waiting with her army of teachers for the mother-daughter duo at the bus stand. They had done their LT together. Shanti was Sharda Khanna's maternal aunt's daughter. When she took the two of them to her bungalow, Rajrajeshwari felt she couldn't move for a moment, as if somebody had shackled her legs.

'This is such a beautiful bungalow, Amma. Looks just like a king's palace!' Chandan kept prattling on excitedly but her mother was being taunted by cruel destiny at every step.

'Yes, yes, what your daughter is saying is right,' Shanti said. The speed with which she took them into the drawing room, Rajeshwari wasn't prepared for it.

'Please excuse me, Shanti, I still haven't recovered my wits from the winding journey.' She plonked herself on a velvety chair in front of her. Had the chair not been there, she would have probably sat on the floor itself. Her mind was spinning but was it because of the journey?

Every chair, every desk, every memory tied to every drop of the chandeliers was like a ghost or skeleton surrounding her in a dance. A thousand memories that she had drowned in the sugar syrup of her sweet-maker husband, that she had left at the doorstep of her household now took aim at her like a thousand spears. It seemed like someone had breathed life into the very picture of the dead king. His moustache seemed to go up, mocking her, piercing her.

'Come, lie down in my room, Rajeshwari!' said Shanti, 'It looks like you are very tired. I'll give you a cup of lemon tea. It will revive you.'

There was no room in that house where she could rest. No room where her lover's ghost wouldn't climb up on her chest and try to strangle her.

She felt more anxious in Shanti's room. This had once been Kundan's room. She had scratched the letters 'K' and 'R' in the memory of their love on a wall of this very room. They were probably still there!

Shanti had gone to make tea and her daughter, who was seeing the hills for the first time, was running around to admire the swaying Deodars or the peaks of snowy Kamet or Trishul. Finding herself suddenly alone, Rajrajeshwari started walking around the room, surveying the walls, taking stock of her memories.

She found the letters they had scratched in under the layers of paint. Is the writing of an emotional youth so impossible to erase? She kept thinking of a saying in English—one's first love never dies. That had been her first and last love.

'Here, drink the tea.' When Shanti entered with the tea, Rajrajeshwari was so startled that it felt like she had been caught stealing red-handed.

Shanti gave her the tea and sat in a chair with her cup.

'That is the joy of living here, Rajeshwari!' Shanti said in between sips of tea, 'I got this furnished bungalow for a very small rent—came with the carpets, rugs and sofas, everything. I've heard that some king had had it built for his mistress but whoever is destined to live in a house lives in it, isn't it so? The house was built for a mistress but in it lives a headmistress.' Laughing at her own pun, she continued, 'Let me see where your daughter has gone off to. Let me give her a cup of tea, Rajeshwari.' On her way out, she turned around to say, 'When you wrote to me saying you were coming here to look for a groom for Chandan within your community, I got a little angry at how regressive you seemed. You made yourself independent after having suffered the blow of widowhood and you won't even allow your innocent daughter to finish her education? I was very surprised. The girl has just finished her Inter, such a little girl—and nowadays girls only lose their milk teeth after starting Inter. I wondered whether Raji had lost her mind that she is thinking of marriage at such a tender age. Today, when I saw your daughter, I had to laud your wisdom.'

'Why?' Yet again, Rajeshwari's suspicious nature started rearing its head.

'You madwoman!' She laughed and said, 'Is a precious diamond ever kept by a wise householder in a knot? The sooner you can get this valuable gem deposited in a well-established bank, the better. I have fixed up the room upstairs for the two of you. Sunlight streams in as early as six in the morning and wakes you up.' Shanti was wrong, thought Rajeshwari.

Sunlight reached that room at a half past six in the morning and sometimes, the handsome sleeper in that room was tickled awake by someone else.

'The landlady is also visiting.' As soon as Shanti said this, Rajeshwari's head started spinning like the circular roads of the hills.

'The landlady's daughter is Dr Chandrika Bisht; both mother and daughter live in Toronto. The mother has stayed back, she has come to look at the old house and meet her brother. She will leave tomorrow. Dr Bisht is a very friendly lady. She is as intelligent as she is beautiful. She has done her doctorate on Tharu-Bhutia festivals,' Shanti carried on speaking.

Many hammers rained down on Rajeshwari's head at once—so is Kundan Singh also here? In one of these sixteen rooms? Does his soul also bear a mark of his youth's mistake? Maybe all that is left of that youthful leap are memories.

But was that youthfulness? If that was just youthfulness, then why is it that even after nineteen years her old heart is beating so fast? Why was her face buried in her pillow burning like a furnace? Why was she getting so restless like she had that night?

All night, just like Quinine tablets stuck in her throat, the forgotten, old memories made her throat bitter. The same Chandrika who at one time was dearer to her than life, to meet whom she had challenged her mother' strictest warnings and run like a mad calf, today why was she so scared of bumping into her? She suddenly felt a spark in her mind, a new idea forming. Why doesn't she take off before the crack of dawn on the pretext of roaming around? Shanti had said that even if she didn't get the bus at 8 am, Dr Bisht would take the bus at 10. Rajeshwari got up and quickly got ready.

She had wanted to pay a visit to the shrine of Kaashar Devi for a long time. By the time she returned from the pilgrimage, the landlady would have left. Feeling certain about her plan, she opened the window to look outside. Sunlight was spreading across the veranda. Had she been fooled because the window was closed? She turned to look at her daughter sleeping without a care in the bed next to her. The sun was shining its glory on her tired, pretty face. How many times had she woken up at night to close her bird-like lips—'it's not good to breathe through your mouth, Chandan, close your mouth!' She'd scold her a zillion times but every time Chandan would breathe through the narrow nostrils of her thin, Grecian nose, her mouth would open like the petals of a rose. Even today, both her hands on her chest, she was so fast asleep with her mouth wide open that she wouldn't even realize if someone were to cut them off. In that case, would it be better to leave without waking her up? What if Chandrika came up to meet her and on finding the daughter, ended up saying something untoward? That mad woman can say anything! What if she cracks some joke about Kundan and her? In her heart, she understood the stupidity of her silly fears. Can Chandrika ever say anything so childish to her daughter on her first meeting? But Rajeshwari had been hurt many a time in her life and her soul had weakened like a body that had suffered numerous electric shocks and felt fearful of even a common small hope. Why doesn't she wake her up and take her along?

She had been exactly her age when in the haze of exactly such a bright morning she had run away from home. She had stood exactly in this corner, panting. She had fooled her naïve mother with such convoluted excuses: a teacher at school had summoned the entire class of their high school for an extra class at seven in the morning. They'd all be fed there and they'd all come back at the end of the day, etc., etc. Actually, the matter was something else. Kundan had hatched a plan to take his sister and her friend to Kaashar Devi, a foreigner journalist friend of his was also living there. They would spend the whole day at the friend's bungalow, have a picnic and then visit the temple in the evening. Rampyari had packed some food in a big tiffin box and seen them off on a route that was only used sometimes for funeral processions. They took a detour of about two miles and then the three reached the road laden with black soil. The whole way, Kundan had narrated to her the history of the black road. How the Lohaniyas of Kumaon had come back here and performed homas and how the ones who performed the homas were forever referred to as the 'Lohmi' and the road had turned into ash:

> 'I burned so
> That I became neither coal nor ash!'

He had said this and brought his face close to hers. Chandri had stayed behind deliberately. Her mother's profession had given Chandri an instinctive knowledge of the isolation the two lovers needed. She would at times slow down to such an extent that the two lovebirds would have to wait for her on a hilltop. Every bit of the trudge across the hills added to the glow on Rajeshwari's face.

Today as she watched her young daughter sleeping, she felt like she was seeing her own reflection in the mirror of youth. So many things, said and unsaid, the touch of her young lover's newly sprouted moustache, and two sets of inexperienced footprints forever marked on the long black road had made her carefully laid plans come undone. She was struggling to make up her mind whether to go or not and was drowning in the dilemma when Shanti pulled open the door laughing and stood in front of her.

'Look at you, all dressed up when I haven't even brushed my teeth. Dr Bisht has been busy with some papers since the morning. I thought I should introduce the two of you since she will leave today. I would have always regretted it had I not made you meet this talent of Kumaon. Oh, you have come here yourself. I was just about to take Rajeshwari to your room...'

Clothed in western attire, in jeans, and her hair cut short in and tied in a pony which she threw back very stylishly, Chandrika had changed entirely from head to toe. Had she not cottoned on even after hearing her name? She was swaying with 'western' joy, offering her hand to Rajeshwari as she moved towards her till suddenly it seemed like an unseen dagger had severed her extended hand at the wrist. Her hand hung limp and her mouth fell open in surprise as she said, 'Raji—you!' Rajeshwari tried to feign a laugh but her jaws refused to comply.

Chandrika leapt at her and engulfed her in a hug, 'You have become thinner!' Teasing her, loving her, she had become the Chandrika of old yet again. 'I had heard that you had spread the glory of your beauty at a sweetshop. I had thought you would have gotten fatter after eating Imarti and Balushahi.' Having said this, she became quiet over her own lack of tact. The lack of a married woman's marker and the display of her friend's widowhood gave her a start.

Shanti was looking at this union in surprise. Chandan also woke up on hearing the voices. Who was this woman? Amma had never told her about this friend of hers but the familiarity with which she had hugged her mother and kept wiping her tears reminiscing over their past seemed to suggest that they shared an intimate friendship. Such a flamboyant lady! Dressed in crisp, black, men's trousers and a colourful jersey, with short hair that seemed as if every strand had been stuck down with glue.

'I apologize!' Chandrika turned towards Shanti and apologized as per the norms of western conduct. 'We are childhood friends. You had mentioned her name a few times but I am so stupid that I didn't realize that it could be my Raji.'

'Oh, is she your daughter?'

She leapt and pulled the shy Chandan out of bed and held her by both arms as she gazed transfixed at the face that had turned red. 'Well done, a bowl on a bowl, child, fairer than the father—wasn't there a riddle that went something like this? Raji, till now I always thought that you were the most beautiful woman on earth but this girl can defeat any Miss Universe in a heartbeat.'

Very affectionately, she kissed the forehead of her friend's dainty daughter and then looking at her wristwatch with impatience exclaimed, 'Damn it! I wouldn't have left you today had I not booked an air ticket. Oh Raji, why don't you come with me to Rudrapur?' The next instant, she cowered as she realized the impertinence of her own proposal and went quiet.

How dare she ask her to accompany her to Rudrapur? Would Rajeshwari be happy when she saw Chandrika's brigadier brother's flourishing farms, gigantic tractors, five sons and his voluptuous wife?

'Come with me to my room for a minute before I leave. I hope you won't mind?' She asked the question in English. She bowed and apologized to her tenant and her friend's daughter and pulled Rajeshwari away with her.

Chandrika seemed to have gotten more agile with age, as if she had left the years behind, after having moved abroad.

On reaching her room, she sat on a chair and, moving aside the imported lightweight suitcase kept on the empty bed, made Rajeshwari sit opposite her. She took out her golden cigarette case as soon as she sat down and pulling out a cigarette from it, started smoking.

'Shame on you, Chandrika!' Her lifelong conditioning made a shiver run down the Brahmin girl's spine. 'Have you started smoking too?' Rajeshwari asked.

'Oh silly!' Chandrika laughed out loud and the hollow laugh wrenched the mask of beauty off her face and cast it far away. With her coloured hair, plucked eyebrows, false eyelashes and dried papery lips that had suffered the onslaught of lipstick continuously, Chandrika looked so tired and aged! 'You should ask what I haven't started doing! Children start smoking as soon as they are weaned off their mother's milk in the society I live in and they even rinse their mouth with alcohol.'

Rajeshwari was looking at her in shock. They were exactly the same age, yet their faces were so different.

The glow of one face had been honed by control and discipline to such an extent that almost a decade had fallen off it while an indisciplined lifestyle had inked the other face into that of a tired, old woman who would have leaned on any man's shoulders who offered support.

'So Raji, won't you ask anything about Dadda?' She said referring to her older brother.

Rajeshwari kept quiet but even her silence did not deter the roguish Chandrika. Stroking her friend's cold hands, she started whispering, 'You don't ask a thing about him but this time when I met him he asked about you before even checking about Amma. Where are you, have you really married a sweet-maker? How is your husband, do you write to me? So on and so forth. And you don't even ask about him out of courtesy? It isn't like he has forgotten you! That is the reason why that idiot has drunk himself to a bad liver! One day, he scolded his older son a lot for coming home late. I teased him when we were alone, "Why Dadda, you scolded the boy so badly that he got teary but have you forgotten your Lal Kuan?"'

'He started laughing and said, "Can I ever forget it, Chandri! Given half a chance I'd change the name of that station to Taj Mahal."'

Rajeshwari got up without saying a word. Her posture made it known that she wasn't interested in raking up old stories. Both the friends were thinking the same thing.

Was Rajeshwari the Rajeshwari of old? Otherwise wouldn't she have shown some emotion at the mention of Dadda's name? Chandrika thought.

On the other hand, Chandrika's crass attire, cigarette-smoking and incessant chatter had made Rajeshwari restless to get up and leave. The thread of the past that had been lost in the sky like the snipped thread of a kite, even if she tried to turn back and pull at it, what would she gain? Perhaps this tattered kite was the same as a fragment of her frayed truth.

The wise Rajeshwari laughed and changed the flow of the conversation, 'You have probably forgotten, Chandri, that now I am the mother of a girl of marriageable age. That is the reason I have come back to the hills, so that I can carefully look for a groom.'

'The way you found one for yourself, and your mother found one for you.' Chandrika was bent on getting under her skin.

Before Rajeshwari could say a word, Chandan who had been looking for her mother pulled aside the curtain and came in, 'Amma, where have you kept the keys?'

Shanti came in behind her to tell her guests that breakfast was on the table. The two friends didn't get another chance to parry alone again before it was time for Chandrika to leave.

Before she left, she offered advice just as Sharda Behenji had done, 'Rajeshwari, don't roam around with such a beautiful girl. Times are bad, find a good boy and get done with her.'

Rajeshwari was bristling under the weight of this loving warning from her friends and well-wishers. Will the boy drop out of the sky? But this oft-repeated bit of advice made her more cautious about the future, and the subliminal struggle that so occupied her took a precarious turn. Her conscious self could not understand her subconscious fear and neither did she even try. As a result, her strict control over her daughter became stricter.

She left for Dharchula after staying in Almora for a few days. Her conflicted and tired self appeared to find a moment of peace on getting there. A teacher's family had been living in her ancestral house for a long while but the teacher had been transferred just a few days before her arrival. When Rajeshwari opened the house after collecting the keys from her neighbours, she found it tidy. After socializing with the people of the Shauka tribal community, her father had adopted their lifestyle, and had built his house with an eye for their kind of aesthetics. Teak doors in red varnish with carvings in the Tibetan style, jharokhas made of Shardul wood, and on the top floor, 'Milan', her father's bedroom, was designed in the style of the drawing rooms of his Shauka friends. Everything was exactly as it had been. The teacher belonged to the Shauka tribe and perhaps that is why he had made sure that the room was perfectly maintained.

Mahim would often say to Rajeshwari, 'People praise the art behind the way the Japanese decorate their houses but has anyone ever written a line on the Shaukas and their appreciation of aesthetics?' In designing his bedroom, Mahim had been inspired by the way the Shaukas kept their drawing and dining rooms together. There was a stove in the middle of the room on which piping hot tea was made with butter, salt and milk; the tea frothed like espresso in a brass container covered with beautiful etchings and was then served to guests in silver glasses even as they sank into the plush rugs that her mother had knitted. It wasn't as if anyone were welcome in this room. Special guests, close relatives and close friends were the only ones who would have the privilege of stepping into the sacred 'Milan'. The stove would be cleaned and closed right in front of the guests as soon as the meal was over and into that stove would be put dau sticks. Then, women would sit near it and roll balls of wool and knit even as they forgot their tiredness and the sorrow of being parted from their faraway husbands by listening to the amusing anecdotes of Chinese and Nepalese merchants.

These women had to take special care that their guests were looked after well, especially since their husbands were not present. Raji's father would also go on long journeys like these merchants, sometimes to Tibet, China or Nepal. Raji would come to Dharchula during her vacations, which was her mother's home. Once there, she'd swim like a fish who had been taken out of the water for a moment. Only one kind of crop grew in the entire valley. That ensured that there was no dearth of sweet leisure for the women.

She would spend the entire day rolling balls of wool and knitting and soaking in the colourful atmosphere of 'Milan'. Her father's business had started making progress in leaps and bounds because of his good nature and business sense. Armed with just a gun, he would trade in kasturi worth thousands of rupees.

He would hunt deer known for the exotic essence in the valley and then set out to sell it in lands such as Amritsar or Panipat. He had also adorned the shoulders of an umpteen number of beautiful foreign women with the furs of the cougar and buried a treasure in 'Milan'. That was his only bank.

The house was just the way it had been in her father's time, but it was now more like a museum of wax statues. All around her, standing, as if in a void, were the witnesses of her childhood—the Peepal tree, the roots of the banyan tree, the cooling shelter of the Haraba and the Barada/Baheda, and trees of Dau laden with blood red flowers.

She kept walking in the narrow lanes of her long-gone childhood. The army had cleared field after field. However, a few trees of Amla and patches of dried grass still remained, still standing like the ruined forts of defeated kings. As a child, she would go with huge bands of young girls from the community to swim in the black river and in the blink of an eye her water-borne army would gobble up an Amla each, leaving the trees entirely bare. The memory of the sweet taste of that Amla tinting her tongue black came rushing back to her mouth. Had she got what she had asked for at the Shiva mandir in Tapovan after walking for two miles? The verdant Dharchula valley which was open both on the north and the south was still the same! The Kali River still flowed at its middle, dividing the valley down the middle like a parting in the hair. Right opposite stood the Dharchula peak, lying within the Nepal border.

On getting the news of her arrival, all her father's friends came over to meet her. Their ancient eyes went moist on seeing their dear 'Podpancha's', or big merchant's, daughter.

'Do you remember how you used to steal away Chatarsya, dried salted goat meat and Podpanch caught you one day and beat you badly—and do you remember, Raji, when Rukmini and you drank Chyakti from my silver bowl and you danced till midnight after getting intoxicated?' Rukmini had been her beautiful friend from within a small circle. This one time, she had taken her along to meet her unmarried youngest maternal uncle at the Ramakrishna Mission in Tapovan. Rukmini's mischievous uncle had sung a Malushahi that had made Rajeshwari cry:

> Oh father, get me the proposal for a beautiful wife
> from a Shauka family.

They'd go some distance and then he'd start singing the same verse again:

> Oh my son, where did you meet this beautiful wife from a Shauka family?
>
> How can a girl from such a family ever be married to the son of a Kumya?

This time Rukmini would go red in the face with anger, but Shyam Uncle would again start singing after twirling his moustache:

> I met this girl at a gathering of Shauka families, saw her at the Bageshwar Fair and saw her grazing goats.

Rukmini had burst into tears at that point and stopped going for the gatherings at Raji's 'Milan' for a few days after that. Rajeshwari couldn't go without meeting her even for a day. She had not forgotten the homemade chyakti made of rice, wheat and jowar till this day. The delicious somo is made by wrapping the chyakti in a cloth, put on a pot of boiled grains with 'Balma's' khameeri tikki in it. Alcohol is made by straining that sweet syrup. The first bottle filled drop by drop from 'Jugli's' edge is called brandy—Raji had picked up all this information without meaning to.

'An Englishman once offered us five hundred for this first bottle.' Rukmini had told her, but that man had scolded her a lot later: 'Even your ancestors won't be able to walk straight after drinking one drop of this; is this your land's brandy?'

It was the drop stolen from that bottle that had made Raji dance till midnight. Her friend Rukmini had moved to the Dharchula valley on the Nepalese side and perished there. There were still about three to four good Bhatia families living in the area, but hawk-eyed Rajeshwari had spotted two to three young faces and had imprisoned Chandan yet again. She was familiar with the free and fun-loving ways of these families. She wanted to deprive her daughter of the camaraderie and affection that she had experienced as a child, the memories of which were still buried deep inside her like a hidden treasure. How could she shut her daughter in a room with her discipline? And has anyone ever been able to shackle youth? At times, Chandan would run away even without asking her mother's permission at the slightest invitation from some aunt in the neighbourhood. Her daughter's running away didn't scare her. What scared her was the presence of the well-built son of the aunt, Randhir, who had studied abroad and was working in Kathmandu. Was it her bad luck that wherever she went, all the young men in the vicinity would come home on vacations and roam around her beautiful daughter?

All this, however, was only Rajeshwari's imagination. It was not like Randhir Singh had known that an angel would descend in his neighbourhood for a holiday. He had come to hand over the house keys the day the mother and daughter had arrived in Dharchula. Not just that, he would keep checking in to see if they needed anything and stealing glances at Chandan with a grin on his face. His mother had gone to Almora to take her sick older sister to a doctor and would make sure they had everything once she returned. What he was saying was right. That affectionate and generous woman had internalized every courtesy and tradition of her community and Rajeshwari could also speak her language. To control any person, all you had to do was speak their language. The same lady had opened the doors of her 'Milan' for the mother and daughter duo on the very first day.

'I also had a daughter just like you. She died when she was just seven. I feel like Mansabati has come back every time I look at you.'

Even hearing this did not give Rajeshwari any peace. Chandan started getting invited to the 'Milan' of all the neighbours. But Rajeshwari had seen the free atmosphere of 'Milan' at close quarters. She began taking Chandan for long holidays to distant places or to her mother's maiden home. Her poor maternal uncle lived in her mother's run-down maiden home and made a living by running a watermill inside the house. There was no one living in that house now. Her maternal aunt had died a long time ago and her middle and younger uncles had shifted to Calcutta and Bombay for good. Her wise neighbours had by now understood why she didn't like her beautiful daughter visiting their homes.

One day, the neighbour deliberately gave Raji a piece of her mind. 'Raji, I thought you have spent your childhood in our community and would understand our simple and clean way of life having seen it at close quarters. But I see that you haven't understood us.' She laughed after sighing deeply and continued, 'Our community's fun-loving way of life has got itself a bad reputation and nobody has been able to understand us. It is only foreigners who are able to appreciate us. Outsiders see our healthy bodies and smiling faces and erupt in suspicious anger. We have to do so much for that smile. Please don't mind me, Raji.' She laughed and holding Raji's hand said, 'Do we forget them when the men of our house play with danger by traversing the sharp edges of the hills to trade wool? There are two ways of dealing with sadness. One by keeping a sad, long face and the other by laughing and sharing stories and knitting and spinning to forget your sadness. Nobody would dare lay an eye on your daughter in our "Milan"; even if it were my Randhir, I'd gouge his eyes out.'

The reproached Raji never stopped Chandan after that day. Her old Pitambar Uncle would sometimes visit her leaning on his walking stick. He had also slapped her a few times the night his brother-in-law had dragged his beautiful niece home by her long hair. With age, Raji's face had started resembling her dead mother's. She had aged her parents before their time with her foolishness. But time goes so fast, was what Pitambar was thinking. The same girl whose mother had pushed him to different lands in the pursuit of a groom had now become impatient herself.

'Mama, I can't sleep all night worrying about this girl.' What a surprise it was! She was repeating the exact words her mother had uttered! His toothless smile escaped from under his white moustache and spread all over his face. He felt like asking her, 'Have you forgotten so soon your mother's worried sleeplessness compounded by your foolishness that made her sleep forever after a point?'

'I have to find her a good groom somehow. I would like to get this done by next year.'

However, the anxious Rajeshwari did not have to wait till the next year and neither did Mama. Even as they looked harder for a groom, the daughter, whose future she was losing her mind over, that same daughter's beauty snagged a groom and that too one who made Rajeshwari incredulous about her daughter's good fortune.

FIVE

It had been two months since mother and daughter had arrived in Dharchula. Even if Mama managed to find a groom or two, their details would make Rajeshwari's face fall. One closer to Chandan's father's age, the other asking for dowry. One of Rajeshwari's widowed paternal aunts lived in Almora. Till now, she had all but forgotten about this aunt, but Mama pointed out that this Bua sold laddoos of panjeri and methi and choorna at many well-to-do households. She would surely be able to help in finding a groom!

Chandan had been sitting as if stuck to the fireplace that day. Her discipline-loving mother had scolded her again for roaming outside till late in the day and she sulked even as she sat reading an old, battered film magazine. Rajeshwari was, in the meantime, apologizing to her Bua for her terrible memory and entreating her to find a groom for Chandan in the letter she was writing.

It was severely cold that day. The valley, which was only at the height of 3500 feet and should have been hot like Haldwani, would sometimes turn icy cold even in summer. The weather was imitating the season that was the enemy of the hill folk—the monsoon. A storm of hail had rained down on the stone terrace the entire day. The sky was quiet now but even if the windows were opened a crack, a cold gust would pierce the body like a thousand arrows. Chandan had said that she wouldn't eat dinner that day, that she had indigestion. While writing the letter, Rajeshwari sensed the nature of the indigestion. For not being able to gossip with the neighbours till midnight. Fine, the girl won't die if she doesn't eat for a day. The cure of discipline for indigestion had drawn lines of irritation on her face. She had also not eaten anything. She had just drained a glass of tea and was going to get another kettle going when someone knocked on the door. Who could it be in this cold weather? Outside, nature had started its fireworks all over again. Hail, each a quarter of a kilo, was raining down on the stone terrace. The handle of the door clanged noisily this time.

Could it be Randhir Singh? He would always arrive on some pretext, sometimes to deliver the newspaper or sometimes to borrow a matchbox. And would he ever leave quickly after arriving? If it happened to be him, she'd twist his neck at the doorstep itself and turn him away. But it wasn't him this time. She would have to twist a dozen necks at the same height because outside the door, there were a dozen young men of similar height and wearing the same uniform, with bags slung over their shoulders as if they were Sherpas.

She kept staring at them in surprise.

Had an army group lost its way here?

'We apologize, Aunty!' One of the members of the group stepped ahead. 'Our group has come from Delhi and got stuck in this weather. Could you please let us rest here for a bit?'

He had barely finished speaking when a gust of cyclonic wind made his strange costume puff up like a parachute. Coats made of raincoat material with cotton lining had inflated like balloons. The hailstorm became stronger. Fallen chestnut seeds had turned the ground green and trees having shed their flowers had become bare. For a moment, Rajeshwari forgot that her beautiful princess was sitting inside, and twenty-four young eyes would see her as soon as they entered the drawing room. Her latent motherhood roused itself on seeing the twelve innocent faces out under the pouring sky and thundering hailstorm. Their uniforms had ballooned up to such an extent that Rajeshwari felt that with the next gust of wind they would start flying in the sky. The poor foreign boys at this late hour of the night—how could she turn them away from her door?

'Please come inside.' She opened the same door with great generosity that till now had been opened with infinite miserliness.

The soaked boys thanked her profusely, removed their shoes and sank into the rug in the drawing room.

Having not heard a voice other than her mother's for many days, save Pitambar Nana's or Randhir Singh's, Chandan, on hearing so many fresh voices at once, couldn't help her curiosity. The door didn't have a curtain; she ran and stood at the doorstep. In her excitement, the twenty-four eyes appeared even more innocent and her face glowed. Rajeshwari got up with a start and went inside taking her daughter along after saying something to her. As soon as the mother-daughter duo left, an argument erupted in the old-style drawing room over the beautiful fairy who had stood at the door.

One said, she must be her daughter.

Another said—oh you optimists, why are you building castles in the air? By our misfortune, she could be the landlady's daughter-in-law too! The hills have such young underage brides.

With that a silent laugh echoed. The wise Raji understood that a peal of laughter had been swallowed when she entered the room.

Were the boys laughing at her? What could she do? 'Whenever you are forced to do anything, Rajeshwari' her mentor Sharda Behenji had always exhorted her, 'do it with grace. What is the point of being sullen and irritated in doing the chore? The work can also be done with a smile and happily.' Taking a leaf from her role model's book, she brought out some dried flowers and burning coals on a big platter.

'Please warm your hands and feet, I'll get some tea for all of you.' She got twelve glasses of hot tea with salted butter in just a little while. 'You'll forget your tiredness as soon as you drink this tea.' She laughed and handed a glass to each of them and got up with the empty tray. 'I'll boil some more water, some of you might want another glass.' And she went away.

'She is so stern!' One boy said, stoking his friends' laughter yet again, 'Looks like the wretched woman will serve even the next round herself. Has she buried the girl in the stove?' The colourful question evoked titters that had not died out even when Rajeshwari brought the next round of tea. The rain had stopped, Rajeshwari had dropped a few hints too, but the young men continue to loll on the rug like bales of cloth without a care. It was ten in the night, how could she tell them to leave at this late hour? She was having to pay a hefty fine for her momentary foolishness. When she came to check on them a third time, she found that they had taken their bags off their shoulders and settled into the room like they belonged there. One was smoking a cigarette, one was humming tune after tune and one was sprawled on the floor, fast asleep.

Finding Rajeshwari in the room, they realized she was politely asking them to leave. They would have left after drinking the tea had they not seen Chandan, but now unseen shackles bound them there.

'Aunty!' Their leader got up yet again smiling and walked towards Rajeshwari. She was a little taken in, partly by his clear English pronunciation and partly by his innocent baby face. That made his request even more agreeable, 'Looks like we will have to bother you for one night. Look how the weather keeps changing.' The hollowness of his white lie lit up a mischievous smile on his face. The sky was crystal clear, there wasn't a drop of water, let alone any hail falling from the roof.

'We are absolute strangers here.' He had affected the tragic tone of a damsel with the same canniness of young actors in Parsi theatre companies, 'The commissioner had given us a letter in Uttarakhand.' He took out a thick envelope from his pocket, so that Rajeshwari would be assured that they weren't a party of thieves. 'All inspection houses were instructed to open their doors for us but you tell us, can any inspection house in the world serve such lovely tea?'

Rajeshwari was flattered by the diplomacy of that intelligent young boy. She didn't say a word but kept smiling at him. That smile reassured the boy and he started jabbering away again, 'Please don't worry about food. We are carrying tiffin boxes and vitamins worth two months. We have sleeping bags to sleep in. We will leave early in the morning.' The request was made so politely and the face of the appellant was so childlike and innocent that it never occurred to Rajeshwari that she could have said no. The man with that innocent face was also carrying a bottle of 'gangajal' in his pocket. The traditional Rajeshwari would have thrown him out by the scruff of his neck but she was entranced by that face. His bright smile reminded her of another such young face, bringing to her heart a sweet ache. It was not like anything would happen to her drawing room if twelve boys stayed in it. All she would have to do was sweep away the dust of twelve pairs of shoes when they were gone.

'Please sleep well, I wake up early in the morning. I will make you some tea before you leave.' The wise Raji made it clear that she would serve them tea in the morning and see them off.

'Thank you, thank you!'

She found Chandan sleeping with her back to her when she came back to her room garlanded by a multitude of voices.

'Chandan!' She called out but her daughter really was fast asleep. This was the best thing about the girl, no matter how badly she had been scolded in the day, as soon as night came, she'd forget everything, put her head on the pillow and sleep like a babe. Her ability to sleep quickly like a child beat the enemy in her mother's mind, her fears. Would she have been able to sleep so quickly had she been struck by

Cupid's arrow? Rajeshwari latched the door, moved her sleeping daughter to a side and lay down next to her.

The sound of laughter kept erupting from the drawing room. The vacant house that would seem haunted after six in the evening felt like a house where a wedding was taking place. Her daughter was fast asleep but the mother had no sleep in her eyes. Her house reminded her of the children's story about the selfish giant whose garden would flower the moment children clambered up the trees. She wondered for a moment whether she should give her guests the quilts kept in her father's godown. The poor boys, being unused to the chills of the hills, must be shivering. The next moment her conscience warned her, 'They'd sleep till late tomorrow if they get too comfortable.'

Somebody knocked on the door just as she was about to fall asleep. She pushed Chandan to a side and wrapping her sari securely around herself opened the door a crack. One of the boys must want a quilt. She was right.

Covered in a mirjai from head to toe, one of the twelve boys smiled and said, 'Excuse me aunty, I should have probably asked this earlier—can I sleep with your daughter?' He asked the question in English.

Had Rajeshwari not been a serious and patient woman she would have probably punched the indecent boy's teeth into his stomach, but she had been a college principal for a long time. She had dealt with many such boys who would throw envelopes into the girls' buses and whistle and make vulgar comments. Before government college, she had taught at many private schools and colleges too, and the managers at such schools had not been much better than the boys. She had mastered her anger in such situations and made herself so passive that had someone slapped her on a cheek, she would have offered the other one with ease.

She didn't say a word though the boy had asked such a vulgar question at eleven in the night. Anyway, when she got angry, she could never say a word; her eyes did all the talking.

Her face turned red and her eyes could have burnt the boy right where he stood. He suddenly started laughing and said, 'Oh, I understand. I have been so foolish!' He quickly started undoing the zipper of his strange uniform. Rajeshwari trembled. Will this impudent boy get naked in front of her? She started closing the door in a hurry but by then the uniform had turned into a heap of bamboo shavings on the floor. Rajeshwari saw that this was no boy standing in front of her but a slim girl with an attractive, pleasant face and a wheatish complexion.

'Do you still not believe me?' This time, she aimed a smile that found its mark. She started pulling out all the tricks hidden in her strange uniform and charmed Rajeshwari with her words. Pulling a long, serpentine braid out of the collar of her turtleneck, she started swinging it and teasing Rajeshwari, who was probably her mother's age: 'This is a real snake! Found it in the Gorakhpur jungles. Even if it smelled someone, the person would die a bad death on the spot. Jai Guru Gorakhnath!'

At this point, Chandan sat up in bed and laughing loudly, said, 'What stupidity is this, Amma! Let her come in. Can't you see she is shivering in the cold?'

Evidently, she had been awake for a while and had heard the indecent proposal and its theatrical end.

Looking at her with gratitude, the other girl picked up her uniform from the floor and walked in before Rajeshwari could say a yes or no.

'Now, you tell me, aunty!' She started saying, 'How could I sleep in the middle of so many men? I am the only girl in the group going to the mountain.'

'Don't you feel ashamed saying that?' Rajeshwari thought to herself, grinding her teeth, 'Why did you have to come with these Pandavas as the only Draupadi?' But she didn't say a word.

'Amma, you sleep here. We will both sleep in the godown. It has everything, from quilts to sheets.'

Chandan took the girl with her to the godown where the wool was stored with such familiarity as if she were a first cousin. Rajeshwari lay in bed but her suspicious nature kept bothering her the entire night. 'What if the young girl were actually a Sardar?' But the next moment her intellect would mock her foolish thoughts and blow them to smithereens.

She had scrutinized the girl with her alert, X-ray vision but was still not satisfied. No matter how innocent the face of a Sardar boy might be, there was no way he could have borrowed those lovely curves from anyone, could he?

The godown was on the top floor of the house and the suspicious Rajeshwari walked up there soft-footed at midnight and put her ear to the door. When two girls of the same age get together, no power in the world can keep them quiet. Their friendship may be old or new, but they get close with surprising alacrity and laugh so loudly right from their young bellies that walls could come down. Hearing such laughter from behind the door, Rajeshwari went back to her bed and tried to sleep. It was difficult to sleep, however. She was certain that the two girls wouldn't ever meet again after this night, but she had worked hard to protect her innocent daughter from the new decadent culture that could take hold of her in just one night.

This worry of hers was not without any basis.

By the time the group left the next day, the girls knew a lot about each other. The girl who had slept with Chandan was called Sonia. She was not from the hills either in language or behaviour, nor by the colour of her skin or appearance, but even then she was as much from the hills as Chandan. Years ago, her grandfather had settled in Delhi. Now, her father was running a successful business there. She was the only daughter. She was not particularly interested in studies and so had done a course in Home Science from a reputed Home Science institute in Chandigarh.

'Haye! Are there colleges for Home Science too?' The naïve Chandan was hearing about this strange subject for the first time today. Did one have to study Home Science? Here, her mother was a walking-talking institute unto herself.

'Do you know how to cook without having learnt from anyone?' Sonia asked in surprise. That good citizen had taken two years to learn how to set the table in the western style.

'What else?' Chandan laughed and said, 'Do girls from the hills ever have to learn cooking?' Indeed, she had learnt to cook by observing her mother.

'No wonder!' Sonia thought to herself.

Chandan could learn from her Amma but what could poor Sonia learn from her mother? Her sister-in-law would be abroad six months in a year and Mummy? Could she even boil an egg on her own?

But this girl was really quite something. She went into the kitchen as soon as it was morning. Sonia went with her and stood behind the mother and daughter admiring their skills.

One put wood in the stove and got a flame going so quickly, it was as if the stove was running on gas. The other quickly washed a dozen glasses and dunked a handful of tea leaves like a cook in a canteen and strained golden tea into the dozen glasses.

Once again Rajeshwari was tying her sari firmly before picking up the tray and taking it to the drawing room, when Chandan swooped in like a black kite grabbing one tray and Sonia, the other.

Before Rajeshwari could indicate her displeasure to Chandan with her eyes, the two were gone. She didn't even get the time to think whether the tea was hot or cold or whether it had enough sugar or needed more.

The young, intelligent boys had understood that the moment her mother walked in this flash of sunny beauty would hide behind the dark clouds. All eleven pairs of hands ignored Sonia's tray and leapt at Chandan's like they belonged to hungry beggars. The tray swayed with the sweet laughter of the person carrying it, which splashed all over the room.

'Look at her teeth, Sonia. They look like Mummy's pearl string from Basra.' That same beautiful boy, whose sweet request had won the stern Rajeshwari over, whispered into his sister's ears.

'Why? If you say, we will add this string to Mummy's collection. What do you say?' The sister laughed and replied. At that moment, Rajeshwari walked into the room and saw the two city faces looking at her daughter and whispering to each other.

'Chandan, go. I have put milk on the stove. Just sit there and wait till it boils.' On seeing her mother's stern expression, Chandan realized that she didn't like her presence in the midst of so many boys. She knew she would be reprimanded as soon as they left.

The others kept praying that the milk would boil quickly and the beauty would return to join them soon, but that never happened.

A fortnight after this group left, on the fifteenth day itself, an impressive 'Chev' came and stood at Rajeshwari's doorstep, looking for her.

Rajeshwari was taken aback at first. Mother and daughter had spent the entire day painting and fixing the rooms. Rajeshwari had not been able to find a mason in the market and had decided to do the work herself.

Rajeshwari had given up hope when even after two months of looking for a groom for her daughter she hadn't been able to find one. They hadn't found a groom but perhaps they might find a tenant. She decided to hand over the keys to a tenant and leave. After all, her leave was also getting over.

Dressed in a torn sari, she was washing away the cement from her hands. Chandan was dressed in a pink churidar and loose kurta with her hair covered with a pink dupatta to keep it safe from the cement and paint. She was standing on the ladder made of old, worn ropes and painting the walls with Michelangelo's dedication. Usually, Rajeshwari never let her wear churidars. The girl looked prettier in that

Muslim attire and she didn't like the Muslim family that had gifted it to her daughter on Eid. Since they were both working locked up inside the house and Randhir Singh had also gone back to Kathmandu, she had allowed her daughter to wear the outfit.

Such a big car had come to Dharchula for the first time. A group of children accompanied it, guiding it to Raji's doorstep.

'Does Rajeshwari Devi live in this house?'

'Please come in.' Raji was washing her hands right there. Wiping her hands with her sari, Rajeshwari had no choice but to relent. She could neither run inside nor outside. Her old sari had got a tear in her haste to get up, and she stood shamefaced in front of the lady facing her, blazing like fire in her red silk sari.

'I was right, Mummy. It was this very house.' Rajeshwari looked again at the lady in surprise.

The young woman smiled a mischievous smile. 'You couldn't recognize me, right? I stayed with you just fifteen days ago. You have forgotten me already.'

She laughed again and said, 'We went back without inspecting the hills. The weather had taken a turn for the worse. I praised your hospitality and your daughter's beauty to such an extent that Mother came running to have a look herself. There were ten other boys in our group. They will all send their mothers here one after the other.' Saying this, she started laughing.

'Shut up.' Rajeshwari was reminded of her torn sari yet again when she saw the careful make-up on the older woman's face, a face more attractive than her daughter's, as she stood there brandishing a large handbag.

'Please sit inside, I'll just fix my sari in a minute and join you. Actually, it is a small place. You don't find workers so easily. We have to take care of everything ourselves.' She went inside having explained the reason for her strange attire.

Chandan had been listening to their strange conversation from the ladder. She couldn't decide how to get down with the bucket of cement and a broom in her hand. Amma was bringing the guests inside. As soon as they came in, she would get down and go to her room by the back entrance and change her clothes. The excitement of the plan made her hands shake and the broom smeared in cement fell at the feet of the guests. The cement made a batik pattern on the red sari.

The glorious mother-daughter duo looked up at once and couldn't take their eyes off the lovely face of the inexperienced painter.

Sonia started laughing loudly, 'Look at her, Mummy! Didn't I tell you? Isn't she a beauty?' She asked her mother in English.

It didn't take the mother too long to realize why her son had practically pushed her out in the cold. The same son who at times acted like her sworn enemy and made her heart ache. It had been two years since mother and son had almost stopped talking to each other. Vikram did the exact opposite of whatever she asked him to do. This time he had sent Sonia with the message that his mother should take his proposal to the girl he had seen in the hills. On hearing this, Rukmini had felt like she had fallen from the skies. What was she hearing! Her wildcat of a son had finally jumped off his high horse?

She had left no stone unturned in the education of her two sons and one daughter. She would feel content when her sons came to visit in their shiny public-school uniform. She always dreamt that her handsome Anglo-Indian-like sons, who spoke in fluent English and wished their mother with bouquets of 'good morning' and 'good night', would heap gifts on her when they grew up. But when reality took a turn and pierced a spear in her bosom, she couldn't bear it. The sons got naughtier with age.

Their foreign principal would keep sending warnings to her but Rukmini had closed her ears a long time ago. Her husband's business had opened a fount of wealth in their house. If Gajanan, who had grown up in a poor household, even made an attempt to be judicious about his expenses, his beautiful wife would tear into him.

'Had your ancestors spent money, you would have also learnt generosity.'

She would sing praises of her affluent maiden home and bully the husband she has been bullying since their wedding day. Poor Gajanan was ready to cut off his head and place it at his wife's feet to please her. How could he ignore her command? The house would get decorated every day with things that were not needed. Lakshmi's wrath made the dignity of the home cower and hide in different corners of the house. With age, Rukmini's love for beautification had started to turn into vulgarity. She would dress up in brightly coloured saris with jewellery in the latest style and play cards in her drawing room decorated in the modern style. Her card parties would sometimes go on till midnight. There were few women in these parties, but you would need four hands to count the men here who were half her age. It first started with murmurs but after a while people started talking about Rukmini's offensive behaviour openly. She was still affluent enough, however, to shut the mouth of any detractor with a handful of coins.

Her daughter Sonia returned home like a bad egg with a litany of incomplete schooling in three-four schools. The school where both her brothers were studying was known for the quality of its higher education. The fee given in annual instalments was impossible for common parents to pay but for those who could, it was like a golden insurance policy for the future. Tea garden jobs where you found both women and money or Burma Shell, or a plum foreign job or managerial positions in industries—all these were served by the distinguished public school on a platter to its students.

It was for this reason that Chandragupta, Rukmini's older son, didn't face any problem in getting a high-paying job. Rukmini had found a daughter-in-law from among her own circle, but that guinea had turned out to be a bad coin. Rukmini had chosen her son's bride with a lot of care. The sons she had educated in English schools, who laughed in English, whose un-Indian pronunciation of Hindi words she had laughed at and told stories of, could they ever like girls who had been educated in Hindi-medium schools? It was for this reason that her first criterion was that before entering her house, the girl should furnish her with a convent school marksheet. Her older daughter-in-law had fulfilled this criterion with great ease. She had studied at Shimla's Taar Hall, which ticked her checklist. The second criterion was that the girl must be beautiful. Sumita overcame this hurdle with great ease again. The girl might not have been a raving beauty but was attractive; though her attractiveness was in part because of her father's wealth, in part because of her good education and also because of her ability to do excellent make-up.

However, within six months of the marriage Rukmini realized that in spite of fulfilling both criteria, the bride's father had cheated her like a clever merchant. Sumita was quick to anger, she pranced around like a wild horse, sometimes threw Chandra out of the room in the middle of the night. When she would come back from her card parties, she would often find her sharp and smart son reading a book in the corridor like a tame dog with its tail tucked between its legs.

'Why are you here in this cold? Why are you not reading in your own room?'

'Oh Mummy, I can read anywhere I want.' Her innocent lamb of a son would try to calm her by tickling her with his humour. 'Actually, Sumita can't sleep when the light is on, so I am reading here.'

But gradually, Rukmini understood everything. Dressed in jeans and a jersey, her daughter-in-law would smoke in front of her and she could not say a word. Weren't her own actions coming back to mock her? When she used to come back late from her card parties, she would find her husband asleep without having eaten anything in her absence. The fatigue of long business trips, staying nights at foreign hotels, travelling without any routine and his wife's disinterest would drown him in deep sleep till ten in the morning. By now, both husband and wife had become used to each other's disinterest. How could she say anything to her daughter-in-law? Her mother-in-law's regular foreign trips had made Sumita even more courageous. She had no fear of her mother-in-law or any care for her father-in-law's reputation. One son was studying in the same school that her husband had gone to and the daughter in hers. Sometimes, on their sports day, Sumita would wear one of her expensive saris, put on sunglasses and stand with pride in the middle of those parents who like her had not breastfed their children but done their health a world of good by feeding them Farex.

Sometimes, when there was a cold war between mother-in-law and daughter-in-law, the younger son, Vikram would take his sister-in-law's side.

'Why don't you say anything to that shameless hussy?' Rukmini had once scolded Vikram, 'She walks around shamelessly in jeans in front of your father!'

'So what, Mummy! It's not like she is roaming around naked. In fact, I think jeans should be made the national dress of Indians. At least, the knees are covered. Besides, if your Sonia can roam around in jeans in front of father, why can't Bhabhi?'

How could Rukmini counter that? On top of that, ever since Narendra with his paan-stained smile tucked under a bushy moustache had started visiting her in her drawing room, her blunt son had become even more brusque and started rebelling. Narendra was Rukmini's distant maternal cousin. But Vikram's keen eye could not be fooled by this distant relationship for too long. This distant maternal cousin, who would visit without invitation and use his things without asking permission, angered him to no end. Narendra would sometimes shave with his electric shaver, smear his imported aftershave, of which only a drop should be used at a time, like an idiot, and irritate Vikram with his terrible English. Vikram would sometimes scold him in front of his mother but Narendra had a thick hide. He would tease Vikram more by spraying some of Vikram's Eau de Cologne on his rhino-like hide.

Sonia had also become very familiar with him. This indiscipline at home had made the son rebellious again. Flowing in this feeling of rebellion, he would sometimes invite a dozen of his foreign friends home for dinner and his room would then become worse than a pig-sty. His servant from the hills, Ram Singh, would be crushing bhang in one corner and bottles of Indian liquor would keep coming in. One time, Vikram crossed all limits. His mother had her NGO friends over that day, and in another room, her younger son had a 'Jogeeda' event going on with female beggars and white beggars. He had left two-three jobs in senior positions before managing to hang on at the fourth one that his father had found for him. He had gone with the hill-bound group after taking a long leave with the aim of leaving this job as well and found this beauty there. In the meantime, the atheist Rukmini was turning devout by keeping fasts and praying in the hope of getting her lost son back.

She found herself enchanted by this suitable candidate who had been raised in a traditional family from the hills. The naturally rosy complexion and lips brimming with the red juice of the sweet, yellow local berry. The pink churidar and loose kurta and the pink dupatta covering her head made her look like a smiling, young handsome prince.

Rukmini felt stupid; she had forgotten to bring her camera when she was getting out of her car. Then she could have captured this unmatched beauty on her lens to pour water on the pride of wealthy made-up faces. No matter what, she had to have this gem as her treasure. One, this beauty would perhaps tame her son who had turned into a wildcat. Second, she would be able to keep her proud older daughter-in-law under control.

There was another worry that had been bothering her. Sonia's Punjabi friend Darshan had been throwing herself at her younger son despite knowing all about him. Her face might not even be worth a quarter of this beauty, but her son was at an age that was ripe for foolishness. The son was in his prime after all and his western upbringing could prove to be his undoing. Now, she would not have to worry about Darshan.

'Ay Idiot!' Sonia chirped again, 'We have come from so far to meet you and you are carrying brick and mortar? Get down.'

Chandan laughed a small laugh and then like a consummate painter hung the bucket of cement on a nail on the ladder and climbed down it with her back to them. Then she turned around to look at them.

'Take the turban off your head—you look exactly like a stick-wielding Rajput off to play Dandiya.' She yanked Chandan's dupatta off and put it on her shoulders. Then, she took her hand and led her inside as if she were the host and Chandan, the shy guest. Sonia perhaps took Chandan away to another room deliberately because Rajeshwari had just then entered the room after a change of clothes.

Rajeshwari had already partly divined the reason for Rukmini's visit, and the rest was explained by the straight-talking lady herself. Her younger son had liked the girl at first sight.

'We have girls in Delhi, one prettier and better educated than the other.' Then, she looked troubled and said, 'Please don't think that I am trying to impress you. But by god's grace Sonia's father's business is running well. It is partly god's mercy and partly his own dedication. My older son is working in Burma Shell. The younger one, Vikram, who had come to your house fifteen days ago now wants to be your son-in-law.' The charming lady didn't forget to pause at the right places for emphasis.

'He is earning a huge salary at Mahindra and Mahindra. I was surprised that such a picky boy who had never approved of any girl till now was enchanted by a girl in one night. But now that I have seen her with my own eyes, I'm not surprised or worried.'

Rajeshwari couldn't decide what she should do in such a strange situation. Her own experience of a quick engagement and wedding wasn't particularly good.

It would be foolish to take an important decision over a match without consulting with her elders. She didn't know anything about this faraway family or about their son. A groom cannot be selected merely on the basis of a good salary and a handsome face. The praise she was hearing came from a mother's mouth after all. Which mother in this world would not praise her own son? Even a monkey thinks that her child is god's most glorious creation. The mistake of her youth had hurt her soul and mind in such a way that she weighed every word she spoke like a jeweller weighing gold. Her silence was baffling for Rukmini who believed in quick action and quicker decisions. The more she tried to unwrap the layers of the expressionless face in front of her, the more she found the onion-like layers defeating her.

Rajeshwari opened her mouth almost after a yuga—it was as if the Sphinx had broken its silence—and smiled and said, 'I am grateful to you but I will only be able to give you an answer after consulting my Mama. Please understand, we barely know anything about each other.' She feared she had been too abrupt and struggled to explain herself.

The wise Rukmini, who could tell what cards her opponent was holding without seeing them, sensed the hand that Rajeshwari was hiding in her rough way. After all, she had lived in Delhi her whole life. She realized that this gate could be felled with light fire.

'Uffoh!' She shrugged her shoulders and held out her hands, 'Why are you saying such childish things, behen! Have you not been able to understand women's nature till now even though you're one yourself? You tell me, in this world are there even two sisters who know everything about each other? We will get to know each other when we become relatives? Which elder of yours do you want to consult? Please call him! He can ask us whatever he wants,' she added in a challenging tone.

Now, Rajeshwari felt more trapped. Who was left of her relatives? There was only Pitambar Mama whom she could ask anything. The residents of Kumaon, known for giving everyone nicknames, had given him the nickname 'Gadget', for his unmatched knowledge. The tradition in Kumaon was still the same: a person might not be known by his name but would be recognized immediately by their nickname. Gadget Mama would probably be able to satiate her curiosity and give her the right advice. But calling him was a difficult task. She would reach his house after a steep two-mile uphill climb and even then she was not sure which company of idle old men he might be keeping at that time.

'Please don't worry, such decisions should not be made in haste. I will check with him and inform you soon.'

'But I had decided before leaving home that I wouldn't leave without your blessings.' Then, with great familiarity, she reclined on Rajeshwari's soft Tibetan carpet with a smile on her face.

'Please rest.' Rajeshwari laughed and went inside. Sonia came and lay down next to her mother after a short while.

'Where did your friend go?' Rukmini asked.

'Her mother called her. So Mummy, any progress?'

'None whatsoever.' Taking her arm out of the shoulder strap of her handbag, Rukmini started running her fingers through her hair. 'She is inscrutable. For the first time, I don't know where I stand!' Saying the last bit in English she shrugged her shoulders; this had probably become her favourite gesture. Sonia was just about to stop her mother, she had recognized the gesture. This was the famous pose of Leena Dutt in a play in Delhi where she had essayed the role of Desdemona. But Mummy kept forgetting that the shoulders whose shrugging made the halls ring with applause belonged to an eighteen-year-old; Mummy was exercising her forty-five-year-old shoulders for no reason whatsoever.

Mother and daughter were whispering to each other when Rajeshwari brought them tea. She was followed by Chandan who balanced two trays in her hands as dexterously as a waiter. The trays were laden with sweets, piping hot pooris, spiced potatoes and yellow raita.

Nostrils that were used to food cooked by cooks or a dinner of sausages and bread flared up.

'What is this? When did you cook all this? Arre Sonia, our lunch basket is also in the car. Go, get the lunch basket and the camera. Behen, could you please send your servant with her?'

'Servant?' Rajeshwari laughed as she put the trays of food down. 'I don't keep servants, sister!'

Rukmini felt like she had fallen from the sky. What was Rajeshwari saying, she didn't keep a servant? She rejoiced at the thought that this girl had another speciality. If the mother didn't keep a servant, the daughter must be lending her a helping hand. She had such amazing skills: painting, sweeping and mopping, cooking and to top it such unmatched beauty!

'Chandan,' Rajeshwari said to her daughter, 'go outside and help Sonia bring everything.'

Sonia and Chandan came back weighed down and Rukmini put the colourful boxes of egg sandwiches, roasted cashews and sohan halwa along with the lunch basket on the table.

'I got these four boxes for you. Please have a bite.' She tore out a piece and stuffed it in Rajeshwari's mouth, which the latter chewed with disinterest. The sohan halwa felt as if it were stuck in her throat like an unwelcome guest. She had neither the experience nor interest in eating such rich, ghee-laden sweets.

'What is this? You have been standing, won't you eat with us?' Rukmini started wiping the plates with the clean napkins she had brought with herself.

Rajeshwari couldn't say anything at first out of shyness; then softly, with folded hands, she started saying, 'Please eat, Chandan will give you company. I don't eat without praying. I ate the sweet because you offered it with such love…' Leaving the sentence incomplete and without saying another word, she looked at the egg sandwiches meaningfully and turned her eyes downwards.

Rukmini realised her folly. 'Oh, I am so foolish.' She added apologetically, 'I dumped even the eggs here! I was actually very hungry and when I smelt all the food you had made, I couldn't stop myself.' In fact, she had forgotten all her manners and courtesy and was salivating hungrily. The hot pooris were glistening with vanaspati ghee! The pure pahadi ghee, grainy sweet-tasting curd and with that Rajeshwari had brought some Chyakti made from the naturally sweet and cold local water. 'Please drink this. You'll sleep really well after.' And the tongue that had tasted food from many countries was satiated in just one gulp. When Rajeshwari prepared to go to bed after making arrangements for the guests in the drawing room itself, Rukmini requested to have Chandan sleep with them.

Rajeshwari was lost in her thoughts the whole night, alone in her room. It was possible that this proposal was really as good as Rukmini had made it out to be, but then it was also possible that all that glitters is not gold.

Her guests were sleeping so soundly in the morning that there was no possibility that they would be awake before eight. She could seek her Mama's advice in the meantime and be back before they woke up. Soft-footed, she left by the backdoor.

When she got back with her Mama, mother and daughter were still fast asleep. Chandan was the only one awake since god knows when and sitting on the bed like a bundle.

'Haye Amma, where are you coming back from at this early hour? Arre, Gadget Nanaji, you!' She got up immediately to make tea but her mother stopped her.

'Look Chandan, don't make any noise. Get two glasses of tea here. Don't wake up the mother and daughter yet, understood?' Rajeshwari had consulted with her uncle the whole way, and Gadget

Mama had started his research. One by one, like a priest, he recited the names of the members of Rukmini's father's family and her in-laws and even her grandfather's nephews and nieces and surprised everyone. Rukmini passed the Viva exam conducted by Gadget Mama with flying colours.

'Get your daughter married with your eyes closed, niece!' Pitambarji patted his niece's back when they were alone and said, 'Do not tarry. In spite of being a society of simple people, we know how to nab a niece, remember that.' Not just that, before returning to his village, Gadget Mama took the hand of his niece's beautiful daughter and sat her next to Rukmini. Then with folded hands, he said, 'My niece is lucky to have found a family and groom like yours. Our daughter is also like the mountain goddess Gauri; whenever you so desire, we will send her to serve at your feet.'

'Haaye! Why would I get such a Lakshmi to serve at my feet?' Rukmini leapt and hugged the blushing Chandan and after a long time her eyes were genuinely moist. If this innocent, pretty face could bring her lost child back to her, won't she, Rukmini, bend to serve her?

Before leaving, Rukmini took an umpteen number of pictures of her daughter-in-law-to-be in various outfits and poses. One was in her mother's pahadi wedding lehenga and dupatta, and another in the pink churidaar-dupatta with her hair tied in a turban and a bucket of cement and broom in her hand; she even made her stand on the same ladder as she clicked the camera button. Her excitement even moved Rajeshwari. She had once knitted a stylish outfit which she now ran and dressed her daughter in. When Chandan came out dressed in this unique outfit, the excited Sonia whistled like a boy. 'Mummy, here is a real glamour girl!' For a moment, even Rukmini left the camera hanging around her neck and stood admiring the unique beauty, capturing her with her eyes.

The magic of the stylish outfit and to top it, the magical persona of the one wearing it! A deep maroon Chyung with vertical stripes and loose half sleeves that looked like the kurta of a fakir, tied together on top with the unnecessary pleats of the kurta, a Rakalcha or waistcoat, underneath a knee-length deep blue nun-like skirt the diagonal stripes and blue colour of which contrasted with the stripes and colour of the upper garment. Ornamented with the handiwork and knitting designs of the uneducated Bhotiya women, this unique garment would have sold for a lot in markets abroad where only Benaras Silks or Lucknow Chikan were famous.

Rukmini had forgotten to click the camera for a minute. On Chandan's feet were Bokch rolled up to the knees and embroidered like Tibetan shoes, good enough to defeat the handiwork of any Hungarian artist. On the head was a strange, burqa-like twelve-knotted cloth with the German print Chukti, the whiteness of its Daura making her look like a Dutch beauty. Around her neck were her mother's Karela and a two-string Moong necklace.

'Listen, can you get a similar dress made for me as well? Please…' Sonia said.

'The girls in our drama society in Delhi will go wild when they see it.'

'But this is not available for sale, Beti.' Rajeshwari said. 'The women here knit this over four to five months. Even I took five months to make it.'

'So, can you knit carpets and rugs?' Rukmini couldn't help but ask.

'I have been born and raised in Dharchula.' Rajeshwari laughed and said. 'Girls who can't knit or make carpets and rugs are considered untalented here.'

There was no artifice or vulgarity in the way she said it.

After taking the pictures, Rukmini took both of Rajeshwari's hands and shook them. Then, she bent down double in gratitude, 'I can't tell you how joyous these two days and the happy stay in your home have been. God willing, we will be here again next month itself on our second visit. All we want is your talented daughter. Just put haldi on your daughter's hands and send her to us.' Laughing, she drove away, leaving her samdhin covered in a cloud of dust and surprise.

Will her innocent lamb-like daughter be able to adjust in the strange environment with a fluent English-speaking, car-driving modern mother-in-law? The lamb couldn't even eat in front of unknown guests, leave alone know how to use knife and fork.

Rukmini had said many times that all she wanted was the girl and that they had no need for material things. But Rajeshwari had the means and she was the daughter's mother after all! Which mother could send her daughter off with just haldi on her hands? If nothing else, she would have to send her with a tola of gold.

Her samdhin's assurances were not in vain. She wrote a long letter soon after she reached home saying that the date for the wedding was falling on the fifteenth and there were no auspicious dates after that. She added that Rajeshwari need not worry about anything. She had found a bungalow for her to give her daughter away in. She would get everything ready by the time she reached. Rajeshwari should just arrive with the bride and her relatives. The proud Rajeshwari did not agree with this proposal. She gave her daughter away from her home. The familiar, smiling faces of the eleven members of the mountain-bound group were once again in her house. Her respectable samdhi did not let the weight of any expense fall on her shoulders; in fact, he brought a dozen cooks, servants and utensils in two cars to feed the wedding guests.

Rajeshwari came back to her room right after seeing Chandan off.

Chandan was gone, her innocent pretty Chandan, who was untouched by the shadow of the cruel world. She had no inkling of its ruses. Was this her intelligence or foolishness! If the mother-in-law were so modern, would the son be pure as milk?

She had spotted the empty square bottle in a corner of the house soon after the wedding. With great skill, she had hidden it under her pallu and kept it behind a sack of wheat. Her younger sister-in-law had eyes even on her back. Not just that, when the eleven boys came to bid her farewell, her sharp, untainted nose had caught the smell they had tried to hide under mouthfuls of elaichi and paan.

Will this unfamiliar groom who was drinking even on his wedding day be able to keep her innocent daughter happy?

But she forgot everything when she lifted her daughter's veil during the aarti to apply a tika on her forehead and saw Chandan's happy, glowing face. Nobody could be unfair to that face surely!

That was Rajeshwari's mistake. When Chandan left her mother, her face was indeed glowing, there were no tears in her eyes, and there was no sign of any sadness at being parted from her mother.

Haaye! How soon daughters become another's! She would have hiccupped in spite of herself, but her younger sister-in-law said something at that moment that stung her.

'Do girls these days don't cry like us, Chandan's mother? Shamelessly they leave for their marital home laughing. I even told her—shameless, shed at least one tear to show the world, but by god, it looked like your Chandan was praying that her car should depart quickly so she could leave her maiden home behind.' The jealous devrani was exaggerating, but it was true that as she left her home, Chandan had really looked like she was flying.

SIX

From the beginning every time she fumbled at any step on the uneven ways of her marital home, Chandan's happy-go-lucky nanad Sonia would hold her hand and look after her.

'This is Bhabhi, touch her feet, she is your jethani, understood? This is my friend Darshan!'

The simple Chandan had recognized the searing jealousy in Jethani Sumita and friend Darshan's eyes at first sight.

'To tell you the truth, Darshan had been madly chasing Dadda for the last four years,' Unable to keep anything to herself, Sonia had whispered about Darshan in her innocent new bhabhi's ears earlier. Flicking her short hair back, Sumita had launched her attack at the 'at home' party itself. 'Haye Devarji!

You have brought home an infant. We can complain about you to Sharda Trust and get you arrested. Why Devrani, have you lost your milk teeth yet?' The laughs of the guests made Chandan who was in a red sari turn crimson, which made her look even prettier.

Her husband who was sitting next to her on the sofa had squeezed his child bride's hand lightly, away from everyone's eyes, in assurance as if to say, 'Don't feel scared, Chandan, these are dangerous man-eating lionesses. You have no need to be scared when I am next to you.'

On seeing the wealth in every room of her marital home, Chandan's innocent eyes had become bigger. Such ornaments, saris of different kinds, so many varieties of diamonds and in the middle of them, the shiniest diamond, her husband.

Chandan's shyness was slowly dissipating ten days after the wedding. Ma had written that she should get her husband home to the hills for Dwiragman. This pahadi ritual is performed at the maiden home. But her restless husband made sure that the ritual was completed nearby at the home of some distant relative of her mother.

'Let's go on a long honeymoon now.' Vikram had pulled Chandan to his bosom and said.

Chandan remembered when the maternal nephew of the Chachi in Shahjahanpur had come to India from Pakistan for his honeymoon, that too by air. Amma had scolded her a lot when she had looked at the pictures of the flamboyant couple in front of the Taj Mahal.

'Chhi-Chhi! What was your Chachi thinking when she gave an unmarried girl such pictures?'

'Why Amma, what's wrong with these pictures?'

In fact, there was nothing wrong with the pictures; they were only holding each other's hands.

'These are the honeymoon pictures of Najma's Bhaijan.' Amma got angrier when she commented.

'May this honeymoon go to hell! All the pahadi children are going to hell celebrating all these ridiculous things.'

'I won't go.' Chandan resisted her husband's exciting proposal.

'Why?'

'Amma will get angry.'

'Wah-Wah!' Vikram had laughed loudly and then grabbing Chandan's pointed chin bent over her milky face, 'Seriously, sometimes even I wonder, like Bhabhi had, whether you have lost your milk teeth yet. Why would your Amma get angry? Have I eloped with her daughter?'

'You will see.' Again, he tried to coax her like one would a child, 'Do we get any time alone together till the night? And the damned night goes away in a wink. In the day, wherever you look, there are guests! It has been ten days since the wedding but none of them seem to want to leave. Ok, we'll go wherever we feel like going. Just pick up our bags and leave, get down at whichever station we feel like and get on whichever train we want to.'

And so the couple spent their honeymoon roaming around for a month, getting on and off trains on their whim. At every station one Chandan would get down and then taking her husband's hand a different Chandan would leave. With great care, Vikram made his ever-changing unmatched companion leap from the steps of adolescence to the throne of youth. Sometimes, they would laze under the neem tree in some unknown village, having hung their bag on the walking stick and placed their shoes against the tree. Vikram would sing like a village boy with his innocent village belle of a bride hugging his chest. 'Chhi! Chhi! What are you doing, what if someone sees us?' Chandan would push her husband away and then come closer.

'So what! I want people to see us—you have to be lucky to see a couple like us, Chandan!' Sometimes, he would pull her into the fields, 'It is in such fields that the ornaments of village women are taken and they are killed and buried, Chandan.' He would scare her as if he meant to rob his beautiful wife and bury her there. He would then kiss his scared, shivering, artless bride's closed eyes in reassurance. Some nights were spent in front of old temples, some in dharamshalas.

When they got back home, Sonia embraced her, 'You have made her more beautiful, Dadda! Look at her Mummy, she has got such a tan!' Sumita had gone abroad again. Darshan had probably gone to Kashmir with her mother to forget her woes. Their presence used to scare Chandan, so now, she didn't find her marital home as scary. Though the strange décor of her marital home could still scare her sometimes. What kind of a decoration was this! An ashtray made of a real human skull! Sonia had told her that her mother had bought it for a hundred rupees from sweepers who were going to cremate an unknown corpse. A foreigner friend was offering five hundred rupees for the skull but Mummy didn't agree. On the walls were hung parts of broken idols. Somewhere a broken bust, somewhere separated from the rest of the body was a broken head and on the door with great artistry was hung a thigh with the call bell on it. Every time the doorbell rang and Chandan opened the door, she would blush.

'I don't know why Mummy has such morbid tastes?' Sonia would often say but Rukmini would smile with pride. She really had very morbid interests. There were ten-feet-long pictures of naked chudails on the walls and strands of hair from different parts of their bodies covered the roofs of their house in frescos. In the drawing room, there was a lopped off tree trunk, and in another room, a huge elephant trunk. The lady of the beautiful house had bought it off a king in Tehri but Rukmini had redecorated it to look like the painted face of an Adivasi. Some walls had red stripes or a thick squiggly black spot as if a beaker of coal tar had been upturned there. On top of that, Rukmini would paint pictures on her easel that made little sense.

But the besotted Chandan fell in love with every brick of her marital home in a month and a half. If she ever missed her mother, her loving husband would immediately sense it. 'Let's show you the Qutub today, Chandan.' He would sweep his new bride away in his car to show her entirely different planets and she would forget her maiden home. Darshan had returned from Kashmir by now, and had stung Chandan once by saying, 'Ay ji, doll-bride! Have you managed to get rid of your husband's drinking habit? I'll respect you if you can manage that. That rascal has started drinking too much at this young age.'

'What have you been drinking?' The innocent Chandan asked looking at her husband sitting next to her. Her straightforward question and genuine look of concern pierced Vikram's heart. He felt like slapping Darshan's painted face.

'Alcohol! Did you think I was talking about drinking tea or milk?' Darshan bared her teeth without restraint.

That night Vikram swore on his knees that he would stop drinking to put Darshan in her place and to demonstrate the power of his wife's beauty.

'Vikram!' When his holidays neared an end, Rukmini proposed at the table, 'Chandan is a child right now. How will she be able to look after your household? Why don't you leave her here? She'll join the college here and meet you in her vacations.'

Chandan was sad as soon as she heard her mother-in-law's proposal. At night, she embraced her husband and became restless like a child. She wouldn't stay here alone. Sumita and Darshan were her biggest fears. And then she had never been particularly interested in studies. She would go wherever Vikram went. Catching hold of her thin wrists, her husband enveloped her in his loving assurance. He wouldn't leave her, 'Who will teach you what I am teaching you, Chandan? What better education can there be?' To prove his point, he brought his face closer to hers.

Saying, 'go away', she pushed him. Then laughing, the beautiful student lost herself in her generous teacher's arms. She was ready to leave for Calcutta without having met her mother. That made Rukmini happy. Chandan had indeed been able to tame her spoilt son in a short time. Leave alone drinking, he didn't even smoke anymore. The foreign friends had been banished. Vikram would not appear even when Darshan came to visit and she would leave in a huff soon after.

The father-in-law was also very fond of this child-like daughter-in-law. She would don a short veil in front of him and he would give her a gift every day. Which is why when he heard that his son was taking his bride along with him to Calcutta, he said, 'Bahu is leaving to manage her own household; get the priest to find an auspicious day for their departure.'

His own father-in-law had been a barrister! The latter had given his daughter to him on Amavasya night. That new moon night had not left him all his life. His father-in-law had probably wanted to axe his sanskari son-in-law's superstitious nature but the stubborn knot of the latter's sanskars had not come undone. He still kept some of them safely hidden under his stiff collar.

'Why are you saying these stupid things?! He has to join on the fifteenth and today is the twelfth. Why do you want to confuse him by bringing in astrological charts? What if the stupid priest tells him that the auspicious date falls on the sixteenth, will he leave his job for the date?'

Chandan had not been able to sleep well for a few nights in the excitement of being able to spend private time with her husband again. Her mother-in-law had given her a lot of things that would smoothen her work in establishing her household.

Vikram had a Nepali friend in Calcutta. He had asked the newlyweds to meet him in Bombay. He would book an air ticket for them from Bombay because he was a senior officer in Indian Airlines. The first day of the journey went in fun and games and then started the first phase of their Kaalraatri. They were lying next to each other on the berth after finishing their meal. The train stopped at a small station and three to four army officers got in to ruin their isolation. Chandan was reassured on seeing them enter without any luggage. It looked like they were travelling to the next station and would disembark after two or three hours. Had they planned to spend the night in the train, wouldn't they have carried their bedding for protection from the cold?

Little did she know then that the beginning of the soldiers' journey would be the end of theirs. The train was speeding when they opened their bags and took out the bottles. Then, without any shame, they opened the bottles and saying something in Bangla, looked at Chandan and started drinking. Scared, Chandan glanced at her husband as if to say, 'I am scared!' Vikram's face had turned red with anger. Chandan never forgot the heat of her husband's face at that moment.

'Chandan, come to me.' He said with great pride.

'No Chandan, come to me here.' One of the men who was short and had villain-like thick moustaches spread his arms in front of her, laughing. The other went to the switchboard and suddenly the entire compartment was bathed in darkness.

Even as Chandan hugged her husband tightly, the man yanked her from him. The other three started beating Vikram who tried in vain to protect his wife. They tied him to the berth with a sheet. The train kept picking up speed like a traitor.

'Oh, bald man,' the scary short man said to his friend in Bangla, 'she is an absolute lioness.'

But could the one who had turned into a dangerous lioness on being attacked by four strong men, defeat them?

She could hear her helpless, restrained husband groaning—had they gagged him too?

Will they take his life? Even if they don't take his life, will she ever be able to show her besmirched face to him.

The other human lion had just started pulling her towards himself when she leapt like thunder. If nothing else, she could try and find the door of the train in the dark. She didn't delay a second when she found the door of the speeding train. She deceived the eight hands trying to grab her and jumped.

Death and only death could now erase her blemish.

But even death had escaped her. It had been a year and she was still living her cursed life.

SEVEN

A whole year has passed by so quickly; every moment of her previous life kept trying to pull her back to it but she couldn't run away from the ashram.

Why?

She didn't have an answer to this 'why'.

'Mayadi is an enlightened ascetic.' Charan had once said to her in the isolation of the temple, 'She can't let go of the person she likes. She keeps them tied to her with the power of her mantras. She really likes you a lot. Just see, you won't be able to leave even if you try.'

'But she gets irritated with you, then why does she not chase you away?' Chandan had asked, a little annoyed. But the next minute, she had got angry with herself. This wasn't a question to ask of anyone!

She had never been asked any questions—who was she, where had she come from, why had she jumped off a moving train? Why doesn't she go back home?

That was the joy of living in a hermitage. Nobody had any curiosity or worries! Had the intoxication of charas and ganja subdued the feminine curiosity of these two women?

'Yes, what you are saying is right, Mayadi can't stand me. She thinks I will rob her of her guru; not with the power of my beauty, but on the strength of this rotten body. If I could snatch him, I swear I would have done it a long time ago, Bhairavi.'

Charan brought her dark face close to Chandan's. Chandan saw her ganja-high bloodshot eyes and realized that intoxication had made her bolder.

'The guru is just like a stone.' She said in an annoyed tone, 'I have gone to the graveyard in the middle of night so many times to hand over a chillum to that stone effigy; I have stood there for hours. How can I snatch away the one who doesn't even look up to see me? That Yogmaya knows this. Which is why neither does she run away nor does she let anyone else run. But I have also tied a thread at Paribaba's mazaar. I'll see how I don't run away.'

And then one day, Charan cut her cord that the supreme yogini Mayadi had tried to keep intact and pulled on often. Even Chandan had started shivering on seeing her ferocious countenance. Hair loose, intoxicated red eyes that seemed to be touching her forehead, and in her hand a bare trident! Inebriated, Maya Didi had started dancing.

'Tell me the truth, Bhairavi, do you really not know where she is? I raised that girl at my bosom. Vishnupriyadi was right. She is the kind to bite the hand that feeds her.'

'From the way she had started countering everything, I know where she could have gone. That funeral pyre burning Chandal must have eloped with her.'

'When I think about it, I realize that it's a good thing that she ran away. Priyadi used to say, "Had that darling Charan dasi stayed here, she would've brought death with her."'

Mayadi's guess was right; Charan had run away with the madman. Charan was no longer there so Chandan had to go to the temple to burn incense. Mayadi's knees troubled her, so she couldn't walk the long distance. On the way to the temple, Chandan saw that the tin gate of Shamshan Vihar was shut and there was a big lock on it. She understood that

Charan had indeed run away with the madman. On the fourth day, she noticed that the lock had been opened.

Chandan used to feel scared of the madman when she would bump into him alone so she quickened her pace; just then Charan jumped from a hilltop like the wind and blocked her way, laughing.

'Why, new Bhairavi, you were trying to fool us and run away? Maya Didi has incited you as well? Come inside, I'll treat you to my husband's special hot tea, then we'll talk.'

Today, Charan dasi's appearance was different. A thick line of a quarter of a kilo of vermillion sat in her parting, On her dark feet were two toe-wide anklets; she was wearing a bright red sari and her hands were full of bangles with a shakha and nowa in the middle. The madman also looked unlike himself, smiling in his red-checked bush shirt and black, fitted pants. Having been brushed by love, their dark faces were glowing.

'Sit,' Charan took Bhairavi's hand and made her sit on a wooden stool and asked her, laughing, 'How is Maya Didi? God knows what kind of abuses she must be hurling at me—my food gets stuck in my throat every day as I eat.'

Chandan kept sipping her tea quietly. It tasted like nectar. She hadn't drunk any tea since Charan had left. Maya Didi did not drink tea and didn't let anyone else drink it either.

'I have become a householder after all, Bhairavi,' Charan started saying, 'We have come today to wrap up things here. His work as a Chandal is over. Even today, we turned away two parties. I have refused to let my husband work here. The hand that put vermillion in my parting, will that hand give tea to people burning pyres? Am I not right, Bhairavi?' Then laughing a triumphant laugh, she started swinging her legs on the tin chair.

'He has a Chacha in Calcutta.' Earlier, she used to refer to the madman as 'tu'; now she had placed him on a pedestal by referring to him as 'aap'. 'His company tours the entire country but they are in Calcutta these days. The manager of their circus company is a "Madrasi". His Chacha cooks for him. He says he will find me a job too. It is a lot of fun, Bhairavi! The lioness's eyes are just like our Maya Didi's. Eat and drink whatever you want. Watch three shows without a ticket and then pull the curtains of your tent, sleep till noon. They have shows running all night, so you can sleep till whatever time you want. Nobody like Maya Didi there to wake you at four in the morning with the sound of her tongs. Cheetahs, bears, lions, huge elephants, pythons in iron cages this big! Then there are jokers with their painted faces and girls with thighs as thick as banana trees. I swear on you, Bhairavi, they jump so high in their silk panties and blouses that I close my eyes in fear and start saying, "Jai Guru jai Guru". Eight servants stand with a big net spread under them. It is not like Manager Babu has everything set. These are the things his Chacha has told us. When I start jumping like that after my training, I will be paid a full hundred and fifty rupees a month. Jumping isn't such a difficult task. His Chacha was telling us that when Tara and Mada joined the troupe, they were youngsters with runny noses; now they can jump right through burning rings.'

Charan took the empty teacup from Chandan, kept it down and then started chirping again, 'Chacha is teaching my husband to ride a bike in the "well of death". He says that his nephew is very smart, he isn't scared of the well of death at all. So, I said, "how can he be scared, khudshoshur, your nephew has spent half his youth in the well of death." Chacha laughed a lot.'

'Ai Bhairavi!' Charan took Chandan's hand in hers, and spoke as if to appeal to her, 'Come with us, Manager Sahib will admit you as soon as he sees your face.'

Chandan got up without saying a word. She had forgotten about Maya Didi in the middle of the conversation. The latter had asked her to return quickly. The memory of her instruction returned to whip her. Charan's request had not touched her even a little.

'I have to leave, Charan, Maya Didi's knees are aching a lot today.'

Charan did not say anything when Chandan got up to leave. Perhaps she understood the futility of her presumptuous request. That day, Chandan took a different route on her way back to the ashram.

The next day, when she went to clean the temple, she found Shamshan Vihar abandoned. Charan was gone. Maya Didi had still not forgiven the ungrateful girl. She looked upon her departure as a defeat that had made her go silent. Where had her mantras gone wrong? Had her illnesses sucked away her tantric powers? Who would light her chillum now? The girl might have had many faults but who could beat her at massaging feet, making rotis, getting the chillum to the guru at odd hours? And where would Maya Didi, who was so used to showering abuses on her, find her amusement?

She could not scold Chandan in the same way. And that black girl whom she could love or abuse at will like a dog had left her.

'She will suffer, that wretch!' Maya Didi would get up in the night to grumble and Chandan would wonder if she was going mad. She had probably fallen in love with her mischievous ward in spite of scolding and beating her day and night. Which is why Charan's thoughtlessness hurt her even more.

'She could have informed me before leaving. Would I have stopped her, Bhairavi? Will you also leave me in the same way?' She would wake her up in the middle of the night and pulling Chandan to her bosom, start sobbing.

But Bhairavi did not run away, the one who left was Yogmaya!

Chandan had started taking the chillum to the guru after Charan left. At first, she too had been afraid, but what Charan had said was right! Was she handing over the chillum to a puppet made of bones and skin? He took it from her as if he were a stone idol.

But one day, the guru called out to her after taking the chillum, 'Bhairavi!'

Her heart started beating fast but on seeing the glowing face in the fog of incense smoke, all her fears evaporated.

'You have studied English, right?' His eyes were closed, just the lips of the statue were moving.

'Yes!'

'Then, you have to do something; I don't know Hindi too well.' His eyes were still closed. The smoke which held an unfamiliar fragrance began wafting around Chandan as if in an orbit.

'I will give you some English books, translate them into Hindi. I will also write in Hindi.'

The eyes were closed as before but his lips had started laughing; the guru had such a divine face! From the next day, before leaving for his meditation, the guru would hand over thick books with lines written in red to Chandan. Every book had his name on it in his beautiful handwriting, Bhairavanand! Chandan had been able to read the name on top that he had very carefully crossed out: Shivashankar Swaminathan. This must have been his name once. He looked and spoke like someone from the south of India. Besides, Maya Didi had once said, 'The guru will probably go to South India again—that's where his home is.'

Who was this Swaminathan? How did he fall into the net of Aghori prayers and become Bhairavananda? Charan didn't know all that. All she knew was that Maya Didi had met him at the Kumbh Mela. Maya Didi was a child widow and a Vaishnavi of the Vallabhi Akhada and then had married someone there; when she met the guru at the Kumbh Mela in Haridwar, she left her household of her own volition.

'Mayadi!' Inebriated, the naughty Charan had once teased Mayadi in front of Chandan, 'Since when have you known the guru?'

'From my past lives, Charan!' Looking at them both as if she were gazing into their very souls, Maya Didi had started laughing.

'Beware girl! You have asked me this question today but never again. You foolish girl, does anyone ask Parvati since when she has known Shiva?'

Maya Didi had changed a lot since Charan's departure. Then, when the guru started learning Hindi from Chandan, she became even more desolate.

When Chandan sat down to write after she had completed her chores and the guru had left, Maya Didi would also bathe and sit next to her. She did not use a soap or anything but always smelled like an aromatic bar of soap, as if a package of sandal incense had been placed under Chandan's nose.

'What has the guru given you to write, tell me, Bhairavi?'

And Chandan would translate every line and read it out to her:

'I am the lord of my senses
All attachments have I shed
Even freedom lures me not
Changeless am I—formless
And omnipresent
I am Shiva, Shiva is in me!'

Maya Didi would fold her hands and touching them to her forehead would say, 'Jai Guru, jai Guru, jai Guru, who has understood you thus like an open book?' Tears would roll down Maya Didi's cheeks and she would become still like a statue.

But one day Chandan could not read out the translation to her.

How could the guru have given her these lines to translate? His appearance had also seemed different that day!

'I am giving you a lot of work today, some of the lines are difficult. Will you be able to do them?'

Taking the book, she had nodded her assent without looking.

She had started deriving pleasure from this homework that the guru had been giving her; if the glorious light kept burning before her, could she be blind to it?

She was being taught Tantra-Mantra, Kundalini, Shakti, Kshatchakra, Ingla-pingla, Sushumna, simple Samadhi, Pratihar pranayama—everything by her teacher thus.

She would sit translating for hours and Maya Didi would sit next to her listening to the translation.

'Into the fire which is the supreme self, brightened by the pouring of the ghee now merit and demerit—I, by the path of Sushumna, ever sacrifice the functions of the senses, using the mind as the ladle.'

But that day, she could not narrate the translations to Maya Didi. Her ears turned red. What was this that the guru had written?

'Where could one find another example of such beauty?'

'The very surface of the mirror is unworthy of the face which it reflects.'

'Like swarms of bees flying to the Parijat, like souls of the sages, empowered by meditating on the

Atman, do the eyes of man lay aside all activity and direct themselves towards her alone.'

'Why aren't you reading it out, Bhairavi? Are you not able to understand?'

Maya Didi's eyes became skittish and started dancing. Was she pretending to not understand English?

Maybe she had understood everything. Had Chandan ever been able to refuse any of her commands?

Haltingly, she translated the lines into Hindi.

Maya Didi's eyes turned red without drink or intoxicant. She took the page from her hand, tore it and got up, shaking like a leaf.

'You don't need to write anything from today. Go to my room quietly and sleep. I'll deal with the guru.'

The guru returned late at night. There was no sleep in Chandan's eyes. Maya Didi went to light the chillum as soon as she heard the sound of his slippers. After some time, Chandan got up on hearing her roar.

Maya Didi's voice would get very shrewish when she was angry; she sounded like thunder on a microphone.

'What all have you written for her? Now, will you leave the Siddhamrit path like Mahaguru

Matsyendranath and become a Dhammargi? Chhi Chhi! I will not let any injustice happen in this ashram, understood? I have meditated over two skulls and buried the guru's trident here. Do you think I am stupid? Can't Maya see the downward spiral you are on?'

Maya Didi's roars started getting louder. The guru, whose very sight could make Charan or even Maya Didi quake, was silent. One hand was a volcano and on the other an icy glacier.

'Jai Guru Jaalandhar!' Mayadi banged her trident on the ground and started shouting again, 'Why are you quiet? Swear on Guru Jaalandhar and answer me! I know you are pure in body, but is your mind pure too?'

The slippers whacked against the ground and then all was quiet.

Maya Didi came and lay down next to her after a long time. Every breath of her smelled of the chillum.

'It is a good thing that he went away. You are very innocent, Bhairavi! But it doesn't take too long for something untoward to happen. It is the nature of a man, he may try hard to tame it but it is that of a street dog! Put a bone in front of it and no matter how well-trained it is, it will start salivating! Have you fallen asleep?'

Lying next to her, she started stroking Chandan's head, 'You are very good. God knows what would have happened had it been that Charan.' But then, she took a deep breath and removed her hand, 'I won't get attached any more. The guru's sister from my old akhada, Vishnupriya, is in Delhi now. She is from the Vallabhi akhada but they have all the arrangements for food and Priya will keep you very well. She has written to me many times to send someone like Charan to her. The queen has got a chhatri made for her daughter and given her a house there. She looks after the temple as well. I will have you sent there. You have seen Priya, haven't you?'

Chandan had seen Priya Didi. Vishnupriya had come looking for her guru-sister in this forest. The glowing and fair-skinned Vishnupriya sang her kirtans very sweetly but sweeter than that was her behaviour. But her akhada was in Delhi!

Was Maya Didi aware that her own guru's akhada was also in Delhi!

She wrapped up her daily work in the morning and left to sweep and mop the temple. She got very late returning from the temple that day.

The veins in her head had been throbbing with anxieties of the previous day. At the temple, she had lit the incense and then with the fire from that, the chillum. Her hand had crept behind the idol as if it had a mind of its own. She had taken a deep drag and lain on the cold floor for a long time. There was such happiness in that sleep. It felt like someone was leading her to the skies by both her hands. When she awoke, it was dusk. She got up quickly and started walking. The fire of a pyre in the distance was shaking hands with the setting sun.

'Jai Guru Jaalandhar'—she started taking the name of Maya Didi's guru.

'Take the guru's name twice and all fear would disappear on its own.' Maya Didi would say.

But what would Maya Didi say today? Where had she been and why was she so late? What had she been doing? Would Maya Didi burn her with her eyes the way she used to do to Charan?

She ran, panting, and when she reached the cave, she found it bathed in darkness.

The door was shut.

'Maya Didi!' She banged on the door.

'Chandan, Chandan!' Maya Didi was groaning.

Chandan trembled wondering what could have happened, then she pushed the door and it fell open. She ran in. There were angry huffs emerging from the saffron bundle kept under the vermillion-smeared trident and Maya Didi's injured body was contorting in pain.

'Chandan!' Maya Didi groaned again, her voice thick with pain.

'What happened, Maya Didi?' Chandan held the older woman's contorted face in both her hands and asked.

She looked at her as if cross-eyed and said, 'The wretch has stung me. Went to give it milk and see what it did.' Poisonous teeth marks had emerged on her index finger.

'This was the guru's will, Bhairavi. The one who was once the flower of his sadhana has become a thorn in his path—he plucked it away—did the right thing. Jai Guru, jai Guru!'

'What are you blabbering, Maya Didi, give me the finger, I'll tie it tightly.' Chandan started tearing a corner of her sari with trembling hands but was blinded by her unshed tears.

Would Maya Didi really not survive? Her face was changing so quickly!

'Don't tie it, Bhairavi, a snake in love has stung me. Nobody in the world can drain out the venom now. Don't you see the wretch hissing for his love?

That fire of love.' The fun-loving Maya Didi tried laughing, but the pain made her face crooked and her mouth started frothing as if she had bitten into a bar of soap and was trying to spit it out.

'My eyes are closing, Bhairavi! Beat a brass plate next to my head. Who knows, I might be able to see him before dying!'

Chandan started stroking her tangled hair when a lock fell out into her hand.

Death was standing by Chandan.

'When a person has been bitten by a snake, strands of their hair fall out from the root with just a touch.' Charan had told her, 'Know then that the person will not survive.'

Maya Didi's big eyes were blinking. With trembling hands, Chandan beat the brass plate, trying to wake her up in vain.

'Maya Didi!' She started shaking her by the shoulder. The glow on the slack face returned like the light of a dying lamp.

The contorting body of Maya Didi roused the innocent Chandan and she sat up straight. Maya Didi's body was shaking violently. Chandan's widowed Bua in Jageshwar used to shake like this. Even the hint of chhua-chhoot or any impurity by touch would make her seem like a possessed woman. She would take a burning coal from her mother's stove and chew it like a betel nut.

Maya Didi's fearful countenance shook Chandan's. The face had turned blue, on the mouth a frothy, crooked smile had emerged, and her eyes were like burning cinders in ash. It seemed like she could not even see Chandan who was sitting in front of her. Her eyes seemed to be set on some unseen statue.

'Anandswaroopini, Buddhiswaroopa is Shakti herself. Light and dark—she is the dark and daylight, she is death and she is the beauty of stars shining like a thousand smiling beauties, the beauty of a virgin and the company of a companion! Guru, do I remember everything?'

She lost herself to the happiness of some unknown vanity and rolled back on Chandan's lap. Who could say that Maya Didi was unlettered? She was saying such things! But the clock was ticking and the danger of the venom was increasing with every passing moment. She could not be saved just by banging the brass plate. But what could Chandan do? Where could she go, leaving her alone? The guru never came back so early, and he had not returned since Maya Didi had shouted at him.

It was possible that he would never return.

But the guru came back early that day. Had he been able to sense the unfortunate event that had occurred in his absence with his yogic powers?

The deep lines on his face softened as soon as he saw Chandan sitting like a statue.

He knelt next to her without saying a word. He caught the hand of the body lying in her arms in his tight grasp.

'Maya, Maya!' He leaned over the lifeless, blue face and called out. Then dejected, he sat down.

A lock of his dried hair touched Chandan's chin but she kept sitting, unmoving.

Will this strange Aghori not even enquire what happened to Mayadi? He only kept checking her pulse.

'Did she say anything before losing consciousness?' The guru's voice seemed to be echoing in some faraway forest.

Chandan was quiet.

How could she relay Maya Didi's message?

'The guru had told me the story of Prabodh Chandrodaya near this very incense, Bhairavi!' So saying, Maya Didi had told her to ask him a question, 'My Kaulacharya, in the end, did you make the new Bhairavi Parvati?'

'Do not let him turn into Kapalik Guru Bhairavananda, Bhairavi—run away, go somewhere far away, very far.'

Could she tell the guru all this?

Even Maya Didi's sandalwood-smeared chest had started turning purple. She was still breathing but each breath was laboured.

'It was my mistake, Maya.' The guru started mumbling, 'I knew this would happen some day. This wouldn't have happened had I left him in the forest a fortnight ago.'

The guru slid Maya Didi's head into his lap carefully and then started mumbling in some unknown language.

The tired veins of his dusky face seemed to stand up and then, tired, his head would slump over Maya Didi's face.

Was he trying to take the venom in her body into his throat?

He kept chanting his mantras for a long time; Maya Didi had stopped breathing. The guru awoke at last from what seemed like a loving trance.

'Bhairavi!' He called out to Chandan without looking at her, as if she too had witnessed the defeat of his sadhana wrought by the deformity in his heart.

'It is summer. It is not right to keep a dead body for this long. I cannot burn her pyre, we'll have to take her far away to give her a jal samadhi. The water in the ditch is not that deep, her body will have to be immersed in the Ajeya or the Ichamati River. I hope you won't be scared alone?'

That attractive face held a yearning softness yet again.

An unknown fear grabbed Chandan by the throat.

'No.' She said in a firm voice.

'Fine then, I'll be late, don't worry, close the door from inside.'

He slung Maya Didi's lifeless body over his shoulder like it was a piece of cloth wrung dry. Then, taking the hissing bundle in another hand, he said, 'I will give jal samadhi to the biting attacker along with the bitten body.'

Then, as if seeing something in the distance, that Aghori started laughing and taking long strides raced out.

Chandan leapt and latched the door shut.

Uff, the guru's countenance was so fearsome! He looked like Shiva with Daksha's daughter slung over his shoulder, out to end the world.

'I hope you won't get scared, Bhairavi?'

She had recognized that expression. The woman who had once embraced her husband among Arhar fields recognized that expression from a long time ago. Vikram had left her in the fields to get his camera which he had forgotten near the well, and had asked her the question with that same expression on his face, 'You won't get scared alone, Chandan?'

She trembled.

'Don't let any injustice happen here, Bhairavi!' That was Maya Didi's last command.

Where was the time to think? Maya Didi's clothes were her suitcase, bank, everything. Taking out a bundle of notes from it, Chandan tucked them in her waist; then she searched for Vishnupriyadi's letter; she would have to inform her as well. Maya Didi kept her Nepalese Bhujali under her pillow; when she took it out and tried stuffing it in her waist, she felt herself go still with remorse. The one whose body had not even been immersed yet, her dasi was robbing her and running away.

But Maya Didi, you were the one to command me, 'Run away, Bhairavi, far, very far.' She was stunned when she tried to open the door after reassuring herself thus, but failed to do so.

The door was closed from outside as well!

Was the guru not convinced after ordering her to bolt the door from inside? He had made her a prisoner! She opened the window and looked outside. She hesitated once after checking the height she would have to climb down, then she tied one end of Maya Didi's sari to a nail and the other to her waist and slithered down like a wild cat.

The same sari that had pulled her from death, had now given her freedom too.

Undoing the knot around her waist, she looked at the window one last time and then started running. The guru could catch her at any turn. Panting, she reached the mazaar and found a small magical lamp burning in the middle of the night in the forest. The aroma of the incense burning in it fanned the exhausted Chandan, bathed as she was in her sweat.

Who had burned a lamp and incense in this forest so late in the night? Was this also the miracle of a devotee's faith? Chandan got gooseflesh. The shadows of the colourful threads tied in the mazaar seemed to be stirring in the wavering light of the lamp.

Chandan knelt down; tearing a sliver from one end of her sari, she tied it to the foot of the mazaar. Eyes closed, her lips moved in a silent prayer and then smiling with great self-confidence, she got up.

A winding path straightened from the mazaar to Taalit. She would get into whichever train she found there.

'We'll just take off, Chandan!' Somebody had said to her once, 'we'll get down at whichever station catches our fancy and get on any train that we want to.' Was it Vikram whispering in her ear?

Out of breath and tremulous, she got into the ladies' compartment of the train waiting at the station.

EIGHT

Dawn had barely spread its arms around the world; the train started moving as soon as she sat down, as if it had been waiting for her. Till now the forest-girl had been unconcerned about the absence of her blouseless outfit, she started when she saw the other women in the compartment. A group that had been to a fair filled her compartment. She suddenly became aware of her immodest attire among them. Chhi-Chhi! What would people say when they saw her state of semi-nakedness? She wrapped her saffron sari all around her hands and face.

Neither did she have a ticket nor a travelling companion. She sat down in a corner like a saffron bundle. As soon as the train started, a heated verbal duel broke out between two villagers returning from the fair. The attention that had been momentarily fixed on her, was now focused on this new source of entertainment. The fight got over only when the group's destination arrived. Chandan was now all alone in the compartment.

In her loneliness, she remembered with sadness another such train ride. Those fierce faces, the four demons surrounding her like dogs and the groans of her husband calling out to her, 'Chandan, Chandan!' Vikram had seen her ruination, then how could she dare tie a thread at the mazaar?

For a moment, she wanted to alight, run back, untie the thread and let it float away in the air. The train seemed to be ambling along, saluting every station. Nobody entered the compartment, and nobody came to check her ticket. The moment she felt that a station was nearing, she would run into the toilet and bolt the door, but how long could she play this game of hide and seek?

The unknown destination arrived ultimately, and her compartment was isolated as it stood still in the yard. All was quiet. Feeling fearful, she stepped out of the train from the back door. She did not hesitate to jump out when she saw the small iron door unguarded.

When she stepped out, the familiar city snatched her saffron clothes off her and rendered her completely naked.

'Try as hard as you might want to, new Bhairavi, will you be able to hide from us?'

Trucks loaded with iron rods, black and yellow taxis, colourful cars and scooters. She stood shocked in the middle of the milling crowd like a village belle lost at a fair.

'Oh, new Bhairavi, where are you coming from?'

Vishnupriya Didi, saffron bedding on her head, took her hand.

'Have you come alone or has Maya come with you? It's good that we met here, have you forgotten your luggage in the train?' Chandan could not answer any of Priyadi's many questions.

From the expression on Chandan's face, the wise Vaishnavi understood that something unfortunate had happened.

'Let me call a taxi, you look very tired, you'll get more tired on a bus. I stopped taking scooters since the time I fell from one.'

Chattering thus by herself, Vishnupriya Didi hailed a taxi and they settled in.

'It's good that I returned today, otherwise you would have kept looking for me everywhere.

I had taken Raniji to Mathura, Vrindavan and then Nathdwara. Raniji remained there, saying, "Vishnupriya, you should go, my Radhagovind is all by himself there." So I came back. She doesn't let the gates of the temple close for more than eight days. I was wondering how I would live alone. Govind sent you, thankfully.' The fatigue from the journey entered the eyes that hadn't slept for two nights. Without saying anything and with a sad expression, Chandan continued to look out of the speeding taxi.

Vishnupriya Didi asked the taxi driver to stop when they reached their destination and taking her bedding roll out of the car laughed and said to Chandan, 'Won't you get out?'

The Radhagovind temple was on the western side of Raniji's enormous haveli and Vishnupriya Didi lived in its storeroom.

'Why Bhairavi, your silence is frightening. Is everything fine? I haven't received any letters from Maya in a while. Is Maya fine?'

Would she have come here had Maya been fine? The tears she had been trying so hard to hold back started flowing and told the truth. Then, Chandan dried her eyes. Haltingly, she told Vishnupriya everything. Vishnupriya was Maya Didi's guru behen. Had Maya Didi been alive, she would have told her everything herself. The pain Chandan had been holding back for so long poured out of her.

'I knew that unfortunate wretch would come to such an end some day! She left a Vaishnavi akhada to give company to snakes. That Aghori demon had bewitched her!' Vishnupriya dried her eyes with the end of her sari and took a long breath.

'Now, where will you go, Bhairavi?'

This jolted Chandan out of her sad reverie; she was not prepared for such a question.

Vishnupriya did not have the courage to keep this spark of beauty in her arsenal. Raniji's young nephew visited often with his friends. Even Vishnupriya's guru came on visits. The one whose divine beauty had swayed Maya's learned master could just as well make her old guru dream of the hues of happiness.

It was clear to Chandan that Vishnupriya was reluctant to make her a member of her akhada because she had run away from the last one. Vishnupriya had brought her from the station thinking that a student of Maya's had come to visit Delhi. Chandan got up without answering the question she had been asked twice now.

'I'll leave now, Priyadi!' She pulled her saffron sari to her shoulder.

It was pitch dark partly because it was almost dusk and partly because of an overcast sky. It looked like it might rain any time.

'Oh Ma! Where will you go in this new city? That too with this face. Here, even old Vaishnavis are harassed by louts and you…?' Chandan stopped her mid-sentence, laughed and said, 'Don't worry about my face, Priyadi. I have learnt to hide it well.'

Indeed, she wrapped the sari around herself, turning it into a burqa.

'See?' She said in a strangled voice, 'Now, who can tell whether it is a Sanyasi or a Sanyasini?' She left as Priya looked on at her retreating back. Thank god, the problem had been resolved on its own.

Clad in her saffron attire, Chandan went to the bus stop and waited there. She had stood at this very bus stop with Sonia and Vikram so many times. The tall building with blinking lights which said LIC brought back so many memories. When she had not made a mistake in alighting where she had, then how could she make a mistake in recognizing this huge building?

She had a cup of tea at a tea shop on the road. Then pulling the chillum out from her waist, she filled it and asked the shopkeeper for four burning coals; he looked shocked. Her entire face was covered, just her eyes could be seen. The sanyasi had covered his face so! Maybe he was suffering from a terrible disease, his nose might have fallen off and he had covered his face in that saffron robe to hide the grotesqueness of his visage. Delhi was full of such specimens.

The shopkeeper took four burning coals from his stove and dropped them in the chillum.

She recognized the leader under whose statue she was sitting, chillum in hand.

'If you ever lose your way, then remember, Bhabhi!' Sonia had said, 'Walk in a straight line from this statue's nose, then turn at its left ear. The gate with the netted wall is ours.' She took a long puff under the statue—'Jai Guru Jaalandhar. You've gotten me so far, now look after me the rest of the way too.'

Baba Pir, I have tied a thread at your mazaar; the intoxicating smoke of the chillum was reaching her head, making her luscious eyes look like cinders.

When she got up, neither did her legs tremble, nor her heart. She was now an accomplished heroine on her way to meet her dearest love.

She did not hesitate even a little when she saw the milky white lights shining on the netted walls. Was this way still open for her?

'It is not difficult to run away from your husband's house, Bhairavi,' Maya Didi had once said to her swaying in her intoxication. 'What is difficult is returning there. The door you had opened and jumped out of, will you be able to return to it?'

She was at the back door. That narrow alley, by which the milkman brought his buffalo for the milk delivery. With tremendous self-confidence, she walked in as if she had just returned from a walk. It did not take her long to recognize her window; she stood under it, patiently waiting.

The thread she had tied at the baba's mazaar started flitting in front of her intoxicated eyes.

Strains of western music floated in from another window. The bittersweet smell of Nibori reawakened her memory. Her golden past floated in front of her eyes. Holding her husband's hand at unknown small stations, roaming in the forest of young love, she remembered all of that. Now, she did not fear being seen or heard.

A long car came and halted next to her instead of rolling up at the portico.

Had the driver not been careful, he would have surely hit her.

'Who is this impudent wretch?' He got out seething in anger and stood in front of her.

That laugh.

It was such a strange laugh. As if a person long dead had returned after an age to visit his relatives for one last time.

She stood resolute before him like the epitome of hapless beauty.

'I knew I would get to see you; after all I had tied a thread at the Baba's mazaar.' She laughed again and with this laugh, the fields of Arhar, the well and the Dharchula valley all appeared before Vikram.

'Chandan, Chandan!' He caught hold of her and started kissing her like a madman. He forgot that his second wife had just vanquished death to make him a father. He forgot that the car he had just alighted from and under whose shade he was kissing her madly was a gift from his new mother-in-law. He even forgot that his mother and mother-in-law were pacing inside the house, waiting to hear about his wife's well-being. He had taken leave of his senses on seeing the new beauty of his beloved. The knee-length dhoti, rudraksha mala around the neck, the semi-nakedness of the divine beauty he had made his own once! His wife, his companion, his lover.

No, nothing could besmirch that face. That stain had made her more beautiful, like the spot on the moon! He leaned over her mouth again but this was not the familiar smell of kasturi which he was familiar with, having lived at his hunter grandfather's house. He recognized this smell. This was the smell that had wafted about his old foreigner friends. The lines in English he had read recently appeared in front of him.

'The smell of marijuana clings to breath and clothing. The smokers suffer from bloodshot eyes.'

Had the intoxicating smell coming from every fold of her attire made her eyes go red?

To see if his suspicion was right, Vikram lifted the face that had drooped over his chest and his companion tightened her embrace. She seemed afraid that this treasure she had found with such effort would be snatched away from her.

'Vikram, where did you go?' Startled, they parted. Her mother-in-law's voice pulled Chandan back to the present. She quickly hid behind a pillar.

'I am coming, Mummy.' Vikram moved towards his mother as she stood near the car after climbing down the stairs.

Chandan saw her mother-in-law from behind the pillar and suppressed the hiccup forming in her throat and closed her eyes.

'Why don't you say what happened?' Mother-in-law looked very scared.

Vikram caught hold of her hand and pulled her towards the portico—

'Why don't you say anything? Is Darshan fine? I called the hospital so many times. Your mother-in-law has fainted some hundred times. She is anyway neurotic, and ever since she heard it was a caesarean she went mad chanting Darshan's name. What happened? Say something, son, I am prepared for the worst.'

'Darshan is fine, Mummy. It's a boy.' He whispered softly but the one standing just at a short distance had heard him.

Fate had drowned her in such a strange swamp!

His mother took the whisper and turned it into a loud fireball and threw it out: 'Arre Sonia, give Darshan's mother smelling salts again! It is a boy. Come inside, why are you standing here? We have to give Daddy a trunk call.'

'Look at his fate, stays at home every day but the day he gets a grandson, he's in Bombay.' She pulled her son inside.

Chandan walked out the same way she had come in. Maya Didi had been right, 'Any man can forgive all your sins at just the sight of your face and he after all is your lusting husband.'

The kind judge had indeed forgiven all her faults. Could she still be freed from the eternal stigma of her exile?

Even after being freed of one's shackles, a prisoner cannot forget their death sentence, their conscience shackles them forever. They look at their life transformed by just a moment and wonder, where would they go now?

Chandan, like a prisoner set free was wondering the same thing: where would she go? Where?